Devanshi Sharma is twenty-three years and four books old. She loves talking about writing and has been invited as a speaker to many institutions, including SRCC and IIT Delhi, to judge their competitions. A dreamer by choice and a stubborn workaholic, for her, her family is her lifeline.

Hailing from the city of food, Indore, Devanshi is a total foodie and enjoys travelling while she is writing. Her previous books – *No Matter What I Do* and *Imperfect Misfits* – are hot-selling reads and continue to charm youngsters and elderly alike.

You can know more about her or get in touch with her at:

f /authordevanshi   www devanshisharma.com

0640 644

Praise for the author and her works

'Girl on the go!'

– The Tribune

'She's making the write choice.'

– DNA

'A tantalising read...with soul-touching narrative.'

– The Times of India

'Unimaginably Talented.'

– Hindustan Times

'Dreams as a ray of hope: Devanshi.'

– The Chronicle, Raipur

I Think I am in Love

DEVANSHI SHARMA

Happy Reading

Srishti
PUBLISHERS & DISTRIBUTORS

SRISHTI PUBLISHERS & DISTRIBUTORS
Registered Office: N-16, C.R. Park
New Delhi – 110 019
Corporate Office: 212A, Peacock Lane
Shahpur Jat, New Delhi – 110 049
editorial@srishtipublishers.com

First published by
Srishti Publishers & Distributors in 2019

Copyright © Devanshi Sharma, 2019

10 9 8 7 6 5 4 3 2

This is a work of fiction. The characters, places, organisations and events described in this book are either a work of the author's imagination or have been used fictitiously. Any resemblance to people, living or dead, places, events or organisations is purely coincidental.

The author asserts the moral right to be identified as the author of this work.

Printed and bound in India

Acknowledgement

I always feel that the freedom my mind has is all because of two people – Mom and Dad. Whatever, wherever, whenever I do something, it's because of them. The biggest hug and thank you to them for bringing me up as a person who is free to make mistakes and then win over them.

Tolerating a workaholic writer is a task and my family has been doing that perfectly for a while. My grandparents, my families in Gurgaon and Raipur have been of constant support. To have them with me is a blessing, and without them, I wouldn't have completed the book. I love you guys.

A special thank you to three people without whom my life wouldn't be as cheerful as it is – Soumya, Bhai and Gungun.

To hear my stories over phone, to hear my blabber and to tell me that the next story should be 20% better than the last one, my gang of friends in Indore have just been my backbone and so have people here in my workplace. It's a happy workplace family in Gurgaon and to all those who have been there in office by my side, thank you!

To the best *padosis* I have, thanks for hearing the stories on all weekends and discussing so many ideas!

My reviewers – Priya and Neha. A big thanks for all the comments, feedback and appreciation. All of it made our book great and that means a lot.

A special shout out to my metro buddy, who gave this story an altogether new perspective.

Last but the most important, the crew – Arup, Vivek and everyone at Srishti Publishers. The best editor – Stuti, you have always ensured our book conveys what the story wanted to. And to the cutest and the youngest contributor – Amay. Thanks, little hero.

To all the lovely readers, much love!

Prologue

"I know I won't get an answer, but I wanted to ask something," she said rather authoritatively.

Amidst the pin drop silence, her words echoed in the empty hotel room.

Ranchi, now famous as skipper M.S. Dhoni's birth town, is a quiet city. It resonates the warmth of Bihar's culture and hospitality, wherein everyone is welcomed with open arms. The city had welcomed Meera and Ishaan with the same warm embrace.

These two, I'd say, were like two un-friended friends. Wondering what that means? Well, that they were bothered about each other quite a bit, but pretended that they didn't care. Amidst the steady strains in the friendship now, they had seen their lows and highs. But keeping aside their apprehensions, they had entered Ranchi with seven of their friends to attend a colleague's wedding.

While the rest of the gang was overjoyed and excited to explore the new city in the evening, these two weirdoes sat inside the hotel room, pretending to look into their phones with awkwardness freely flowing in the room, accompanied by its best friend, silence, garnished with anger.

The room was bursting with unheard feelings, unsaid emotions, open-ended conversations, and an orphaned friendship which was hopefully waiting for both of them to adopt it. In a room hypnotized by silence, Meera's words were piercing. But, as always, Ishaan's silence was sharper than her words. He made sure his reply was as wry as it could be.

"If you know you'll not get an answer, why do you even bother to ask?"

Wearing a navy blue kurta, Ishaan depicted the calmness of the sky. It seemed as if peace was encapsulated in him. He lay down on the bed, facing Meera, but not looking at her. He tried his best to escape her questions and her company, but when two people have to end up together, they do. No matter what.

Ishaan did not want any conversation to begin, because he knew well this question would come up. Especially when she had stayed quiet and unexpectedly formal in front of everyone else.

She was always the inquisitive and curious one, and he, always someone who would speak only when he wanted to. A Cancerian and a Sagittarius can be a deadly combination, after all.

And Cancerians are pretty stubborn. They don't give up easily. Being one, Meera questioned, "You feel you have the liberty of disappearing from someone's life without their permission?"

The first question fired and he immediately put his earphones on, pretending to not hear a word. Mind you, no music was playing yet.

Meera had taken off her kohl, but her eyes were red; she had taken off her copper eye-shadow, but the eye-lids complained of sleeplessness; her make-up remover had cleared her skin of all shimmer, but there was a big, fat tear shining on it. Even when she was here for a dear friend's wedding, for which she was most excited, her usual smile was missing.

Like all other times, this time too, his silence pinched her inside out. Every time she wanted an answer, his silence was her reply. Every time she wanted a friend to hug, his quietness came in between and every time she wanted to talk to him, his lack of words answered back. In the race between her words and his silence, his silence always won.

However, she didn't give up on him – she never had, she never would. She came closer to him and said firmly, "Take off your earphones! *Now!*" Her eyes sparkled with anger, and knowing her anger, he hardly wanted her to begin. He reluctantly removed the earphone from his right ear as she asked, "It is pretty unfair to just stop talking to a friend without having any reason, Ishaan."

His face reflected a mix of irritation, expectation and frustration.

'*How do I tell her that if I answer her questions, I'll end up making things complicated for her, for us, for everyone? It's best that I keep quiet right now, although I hate to see her in such a condition,*' he contemplated.

For him, she was a little kid wanting to chase him. But for her, he was her reason to smile.

"So be it, Meera. I am happy being unfair," he replied, irritated, trying desperately to evade answering.

As much as she felt he had an innocent smile and a beautiful heart, she had also tasted his volcanic anger. His face, that was undoubtedly calm usually, looked miffed today. As if silently pleading her to leave him alone; as if silently requesting her to not invite more insult on herself.

But, what Meera saw in his silence was the underlying answer to many of her questions.

Silence is sometimes a strong foundation of some relationships, and words are then, mere spoilers.

Disclaimer:

Meera's world is full of unsaid emotions, half-hearted conversations and endless aspirations. There is drama that accompanies her throughout.

Enter at your own risk.

THE END

A conversation without words!

Meera Tiwari is feeling excited.
1 December, 15:45
New Delhi Railway Station

'Travelling to my best friend's wedding!! By the way, travelling in a train after five long years!'

Meera quickly updated her Facebook status with a bright smile as she boarded the blue-painted Rajdhani Express to Ranchi. She wasn't a lover of weddings as such, but the fact that she was travelling to one of her closest colleague's wedding gave her exciting vibes. Being the most expressive kinds, she immediately chose to let her Facebook frenzy know how she was feeling and what she was doing.

She was a popular fashion vlogger. And with a good thirty-two thousand people following her, the moment she posted her picture with the status, there was a flood of likes and comments. Meera replied to a few comments with a dazzling smile that shone through her lip gloss, and stayed in her shell pretty happily. For others, recreation was in enjoying vacations, but for Meera, recreation was hidden in her work.

She was someone who took time to get comfortable, and until she wasn't comfortable, she was happier being in a zone where she was. Her work was her comfort zone, where people loved her for being herself.

'*What is life minus hardwork and emotions?*' she always thought.

They were a bunch of office friends travelling together from Delhi, and strangely, while six of them were engrossed in conversations, the seventh one found a place near the window. Meera was a rare case of being an extreme – either she was jumping with excitement, or she was gloomy with thoughts. A rare, over-thinking specie, I may add.

Big, dark black eyes, some dark circles beneath them, chubby cheeks, long, black and wavy hair tied loosely in a pony tail and a dazzling smile. As she stared at the sun setting gracefully through the train's window, her eyes traced the landscapes outside. An hour ago, she was beaming with joy to jump into this journey. She had her set of apprehensions, insecurities and fear to lose more on the self-respect that she was already compromising on, but, keeping everything in a suitcase and locking it, she wanted to at least pretend to be excited.

In exactly 60 minutes, that excitement of hopping on to a new journey was replaced by void of being quiet. In exactly 1200 seconds, that dazzling selfie smile that she had posted on her Facebook timeline was replaced by a pretentious and forced smile. To top it, one of her friends commented, "Thank god you are here, Kiya. I could have never imagined being alone with Meera and Ishaan. They would have kept arguing and I would have died solving their issues."

'*... died solving their issues*'. The statement hit Meera's heart. While others laughed it off, Meera's self respect did not let her even approve of this joke. She stared at Ishaan with her big, round eyes and didn't shift her gaze till it had a big fat tear rolling down from them. He noticed her gaze and carefully ignored it.

He knew he could not focus on anything else but her innocent eyes, which demanded answers to many unanswered questions. As soon as those unanswered questions dropped from her eyes in the form of tears, Meera immediately looked outside and wiped them silently.

She had no clue how she would handle the situation she was stuck in, but being herself, she just couldn't let anyone know of her weaknesses. She vehemently believed that sharing her problems would make her appear as someone who was miserable and she could not see sympathetic eyes looking at her. They burdened her with the fact that she wasn't strong enough.

She hid those emotions, she hid those tears; she perhaps was hiding the true self that she was. When you enter a zone where you don't trust yourself, that is when everything starts becoming unclear. Remember, brain and heart together function your body. For life to be slightly sorted, at least one of them has to be in place.

No one but Ishaan noticed her expressions as she turned towards eternal silence and saw the train pass through the outskirts of Delhi. That's what the problem with Cancerians is – when they love, their love has no bounds, and they have already gone so far ahead in their head that they are just unable to turn back. They are gutsy to stay there. Meera gulped the angst and tried to accept things the way they were!

On the other hand, Ishaan pretended to join the discussion with his friends and tried steering it towards office, people and places. For once, he wanted to get up and give Meera a tight hug and tell her that he was there for her; for once he wanted to assure her of their friendship, but he didn't. That is how he functioned. Logic, he said, was running in his nerves.

He always said he did not care; he always said he could replace people and he always mentioned bluntly how she was *just* another friend to him; but Meera was bent on ignoring those words, inferring from his actions instead. Who would consider such words when everything was so beautiful that the chances of what was happening right now were as bleak as rain on an absolutely sunny day.

How she wished that she had believed what he said.

Wiping that tear away, she remembered how miserably she had pleaded with him to stay normal in front of others. She knew she wouldn't be able to take the sympathy of known eyes, the sympathy which would remind her that she was outrightly ignored by her best friend. There were some mistakes which she had made earlier, and now, when she started solving them, he had sworn to make some – just to add salt to their plain lives, you see!

'*Why do I have to expect his support? Get a hold of yourself, Meera, and accept that he won't.*' She told herself as she blankly stared at kids playing on the outskirts of some village the train was passing by. '*You have your work for a lifetime. Let's focus on that. You are independent enough to take a stand for yourself.*'

It would be a convenient option to judge Meera here, but, before judging her, let's know her a bit more. She was popular amongst the youth for her confidence and glamour. Her listicles and blogs were read by over a lakh people daily, most of them in appreciation of her inspiring conversations and pictures. Her work was her strength and when people recognised her on the digital platforms, she felt proud of the hardwork she was putting in to chase her dreams. She was confident, happy and cheerful.

But then, Cut 2 – Here! She was being neglected, ignored and left alone. She had a thousand messages waiting for her reply on social media, but what mattered most for her was to get a reply for someone who had stopped talking suddenly. She got too many calls for collaboration, but the only number that her heart wanted to see on her mobile screen was of the person who would not call. All she wanted was to spend some time with him which was uncomplicated and was just like it was before.

For Meera, just the feeling that she was chasing someone broke her into a thousand pieces, and every time Ishaan was in front of her, those shattered pieces pierced through her heart. She failed to understand that being not okay was also part of the journey that led things to be okay.

However, keeping all her apprehensions aside for a while, she calmed herself down, playing the playlist of happier moments in her mind. Reliving the beautiful memories they had lived earlier, she took out a packet of bourbon cookies and acted beautifully and pretentiously normal to her friends. She offered it personally to almost everyone, but not him. When it was his chance, she just kept it on the train's little table and sat back, eating her biscuit and still looking outside. She knew that just like every time, even if she offered, he would say no. For a few moments, self-respect was her priority.

However, this time, he himself took a biscuit and ate it. Just because he loved anything that was sweet. Could you imagine he ate sugar cubes at workplace? Well, that is Ishaan for you.

'*Unpredictable, as always,*' she told herself and smiled.

They sat in front of each other, but said nothing; they exchanged glances, but not even once did they blink. It was as if both of them wanted to talk, but he didn't speak because he was afraid of falling for her, and she didn't speak because she was afraid of losing him forever. She perhaps was more afraid of losing the hope that everything would fall in place.

Her mind abuzz with these thoughts, Meera got up and declared, "I am going to the upper berth. I just need to rest a bit."

Not giving anyone a chance to stop her, she quickly made her way to the upper berth and covered her face with her jacket, covering each wrinkle of dejection with it. Sleep evaded her, although it is sometimes the only solution. *How many times have you just closed everything else and gone to bed, thinking that when you get up, things would be magically better!?*

While she lay on the top berth, he sat on the lower berth on the opposite side – his eyes carefully tied to the chain of the upper berth. He had always felt she was a kid, who needed someone to nurture and care for her, and even when she had not given him the duty, he had taken the responsibility to care for her on his own. He just couldn't understand that she needed conversations and some time with him and not his care – she was fine being a misfit and she was fine in learning after falling. He failed to understand that Meera wasn't perfect; neither did she want to be perfect. She was happy growing up with life, rather than pretending to be mature for the sake of it.

'*This girl just has to mess something or the other. What was the need of going on the top berth? One, she hardly travels in trains, and two – she sleeps like a kid, rotating and revolving on the bed. I hope she doesn't fall down.*'

While he was dealing with conflicting thoughts in his mind, he almost came to a conclusion that Meera was old enough to take care of herself. He decided he wouldn't even look at her in the whole trip. He thought, *'She is old enough to take care of herself. Why do I have to bother? It was her decision to come independently on this trip, so be it. Why am I being the guardian? Although I know she'll mess things up, but let her mess them and then resolve them. I don't care –'*

Just when he was trying to convince himself that he would not care about her, the train stopped with a jerk, and instinctively, his eyes looked up to see if she was fine. All his logics, which he felt drove him, shattered in front of the impulsive emotions. Once he ensured she was fine, he heaved a sigh of relief.

Why did he care when he didn't want to was what even he didn't know. And why did she care, when she shouldn't, she didn't know. In between not knowing what was to be known, the most silent conversation ended with only thoughts floating in the air and eyes speaking odes about what they thought.

Pin drop silence

"It's pretty cold up here. My feet are cold," Meera mumbled, as she turned and tossed uncomfortably at night.

One, she wasn't really comfortable travelling in trains. Two, she was freezing. Well, with the risk of portraying Meera as silly, anyone who travels from Delhi to Ranchi in December, without socks and a coat, would freeze. Although she had the Indian Railways blanket, but it wasn't enough.

Meera had under-estimated the cold, and was shivering now. She was always the pampered one, someone who would always be taken care of. She perhaps wasn't habitual of taking care of herself.

The lights of their compartment were switched off and everyone slept peacefully, except two owls.

While Ishaan pretended that he hardly bothered, he could understand even her mumbling. He thought, *'This girl and her tantrums! Couldn't she get some warm clothes with her? Anyway, what do I have to do with all this? I better focus on my phone.'*

It would seem to someone that his breath was linked to his phone. *Jab tak tumhara phone chalega, tumhari saans chalegi*

– *Sholay* style! He tried hard to play games, scroll through random articles and read them. He had to pretend to be the busiest man on earth today. The fight was between two egoistic humans, after all.

For the next ten minutes, till his phone's watch showed 1:15 a.m., he pretended to not care. In the eleventh minute, his eyes slyly looked towards the opposite berth and in the fifteenth minute, he got up, took his blanket and covered her feet with it, saying nothing.

She too, was wide awake, her own blanket not saving her from the cold. She just mumbled in the most hushed voice as she could, "Thank you, Ishaan."

These words were exactly like her feelings – only she could hear them.

While he lay back, glued to his phone screen once more, she returned to her string of thoughts. Theirs was a story with no words, yet knitted in a string of expressions, feelings and complications, happily created by them.

♦

'*I really need to talk to him,*' her heart said.

'*I know I need to talk, but how do I talk to someone who has permanently put his expressions to mute?*' her mind replied.

There was darkness all round; there was just a dim ray of light between them. A few metres, a few steps far, but a distance created by words – they were so close, yet so far; they were connected, yet disconnected; they were together, yet distanced by the elegant grace of silence.

When she saw him awake in the dim light of the train, she really wanted to ask him to sit with her and talk to her. She never felt so desperate to talk to someone. Plus, never did she really crave for someone to talk to. She always had friends, family and lots of work associates. But today, for the first time, she felt alone. Actually, lonely. How she wished he came and sat next to her and they enjoyed their time like they once used to.

She had a lot to say, but no one wanted to hear her. She had a lot to express, but neither Ishaan, nor any of her friends wanted to comfort those expressions. In the first look, Meera appeared to be a snobbish brat, a tantrum queen. I am sure, while reading her story, you are almost on the verge of judging her. But, hold on to that judgement for a while! (Not that be judgemental, but if you plan to be, wait for a few more pages!)

I've always felt that judging someone is much easier than understanding their perspective.

Amidst everything, the whole night, she tried to frame just that one conversation with him.

Strange are feelings – a moment ago, she hated him for being an enemy to her self-respect. She literally felt like deleting his name from the browsing history of her mind. And now, she felt like talking to him.

'*I am not liking whatever is happening, Ishaan.*' She knew this would be her first sentence to him, if at all they spoke. And she had re-iterated and practiced this sentence for at least twenty times in the last one hour.

Anyway, that was the best pastime she had at 2 a.m., in a train where everyone else was fast asleep, with a friend on mute and her mind constantly thinking about the person who hardly bothered about her.

While her mind kept probing her as to why she was on this trip when nobody cared about her, her heart told her it was for a wedding she couldn't miss. She thought for a second and then started to rethink about the second dialogue of her conversation with Ishaan, if that ever happened.

'*See Ishaan, let me be really honest to you. I do feel for you, more than a friend. I find a confidant in you, I feel like talking to you, not because you help me solve hundreds of my problems, but because I like spending time with you. If you are around, I really don't need anyone else to talk to, or even listen to my blabber, because you are enough. You taught me to have no expectations and fulfil none. You've always given me that space where I always had the choice of leaving and there was no burden of expectations to stay. But, I want to stay in that space.*

'*However, the way you have vanished out of the blue in cold dust, it's really clear to me that you don't feel the way I do, which is perfectly okay. That is your choice and I respect it, but to still feel what I have to feel is my choice. You should respect it, irrespective of whether you love me or not.*

'*For a commitment-phobic person like me, for the first time, I feel I can spend my whole life with you, and so, I thought I would express it, to escape the regret later on.*'

She made the whole conversation after putting together thousands of scattered thoughts in her mind one by one, but she could not even share a single word with him. The steam of these thoughts on fire created a blur in her mind, which made life look a notch more complicated.

Even when she could easily talk to him, she couldn't. And even when he could make things better, he chose not to.

And that's how the train journey ended. Perhaps, that was the end. Or, as I always say, the beginning hidden in the end.

Meera had no clue what this trip would bring for her, nor did Ishaan know how his immature friend had evolved in the past few months. For him, she was the same kid who he admired for her achievements. He cared for her, but didn't know why. He pampered her, but didn't know for what reason. He wanted to stay with her, but held himself back over and over, and that too, he didn't know why!

All they knew was that nothing was fine, nothing was normal, yet both of them were connected and knitted in a braid as two different strings.

Waise, what would they do for the next four days, I wonder!?

Burden of a suitcase

The other five were fresh and excited when they alighted at Ranchi, but there were two pairs of eyes which looked extremely sleepy. They had not slept the whole night and their mind had been running at an uncontrollable speed, as if competing with the other's.

As Meera looked around at Ranchi junction, she smiled. She loved exploring new cities and their intricacies. A black t-shirt, sea green sweatshirt, a pair of denims and messy hair – she looked as if she hadn't taken a bath for days. Train journeys do that to you! *Haina?*

Soon after, the others also got down and stood by her side. Ishaan looked at her tired face and felt a wave of guilt.

'This girl is stubborn. I really wish to give her a tight slap and tell her that I am not worth spending her time on. What is the need for her to behave in such an immature manner? For once, can she behave like an adult? She has such a bright career. Rather than focussing on it, she is here; stuck with me.' He spoke to himself while others were busy chit-chatting excitedly.

"Let's go! Kiya, check for cabs. We'll need two of them," Ishaan said, breaking the chain of thoughts inside his mind.

Meera said in a low voice, "Let's ask for a coolie."

Her self-confidence was on the lowest rock possible. Someone who thought after taking decisions was thinking thrice before making a request as trivial as this one. And the moment she suggested this, everyone started to joke.

"Of course, Meera! Her Highness has a lot of money." And everyone laughed. Friendly banter, they called it.

There is a common perception that people who like living their lives a little comfortably are showing off. We often judge people by thinking that maybe they aren't hardworking enough. Stereotypes feed that to us. Meera hated such stereotypes and comments. However, for the first time, perhaps thinking logically and avoiding an argument, she just walked with her large suitcase towards the staircase.

Ishaan did not expect this from her. He expected some tantrums, arguments and tiffs between their friends and Meera, but to his utter disappointment, Meera walked off rather than creating a scene.

'I always thought she was extremely predictable. I was wrong,' he told himself as he started to walk behind her.

While Meera struggled to hold her handbag along with the gigantic suitcase, for a second, she enjoyed it. She told herself, 'I've actually been independent through the years of my graduation. No one held my bags when I walked through crowded metros. I really need to be an older version of myself. And, it isn't that bad too. Just a few steps more.'

We tend to push ourselves to walk a step near to our goals, no? Meera was doing the same.

As she was communicating in bits and pieces with her mind while huffing and puffing, she felt a hand over her hand on the handle of the suitcase.

Under normal circumstances, Meera would have shrieked, but this time, she didn't. Sometimes, the touch is sufficient to tell you who the person is. Of course, Meera knew it was Ishaan.

As his fingers touched hers on the black handle of the suitcase, she immediately turned to land directly in his eyes. They expressed anger and ignorance and beneath them, care and compassion.

Meera mumbled, "It is okay. I will hold it…"

As she spoke, he gave her 'the typical Ishaan look' and took the suitcase from her hand. The famous Ishaan look was one of the most disgusted expressions Ishaan could ever give.

Stereotypically, it was the gallant behaviour that he was showcasing towards a female colleague, which was okay. But, the fact that the most non-stereotypical person was showing stereotypical traits was shocking for Meera. She knew trillions of time when she was almost fainting in the metro and yet, Ishaan never helped her out, just so that she could handle things herself.

'*Yes, now, after everything, Ishaan pretends to care. It's just tough to decode what this human being is made up of,*' she thought as they climbed up the stairs.

Meera always said that she would see Ishaan as someone newer each day, someone she would get fonder of. And this day was no different – she saw just another side of him. He got angry, he still said nothing, but that anger had frustration of not saying anything, and this was very well communicated by his eyes. Meera could read the book of his life even when he didn't type a single word; she could feel the emotions in his heart even when his face didn't express a single feeling; and she could live with that love which was nowhere said, but was felt deeply inside his heart.

'Could you take care of yourself, please?'

"Who made a smiley on the mirror?" Ishaan asked as he entered the washroom in the hotel room.

"Who else is a kid here?" Kiya replied with a smirk.

Ishaan for once smiled at Meera's innocence as he stood in front of that mirror and looked at himself through that smiley. He thought, *'Innocence is one such trait that can either become the biggest strength or the biggest weakness, just like love. Meera is a sweet person, she cares and admires everyone, regardless of the fact if they return the same care back or not. Sometimes, she is too giving – sometimes, she's someone I wouldn't ever be able to decode.'*

Strangely, while the conversations till now happened between their respective minds, feelings were strongly becoming evident to the two of them. What's love if not the zeal to know each other a little more every day?

Meera, along with all her friends, reached the hall where

Anshika, their adorable colleague and the bride-to-be was sitting, dressed in a yellow cotton saree. She was getting henna applied on her palms and Meera couldn't stop herself from giving Anshika a tight hug. Just one look at her and all Meera's worries vanished! "Had it not been for you, nothing was worth it. Now that I see you, I feel more than happy to be here, Anshika. I love you," she said lovingly.

Anshika smiled and said, "I love you too, my little one. And I am so glad you made it!"

Even with sleepy eyes and a tired face, Meera's smile was genuine this time. Anshika could sense that something had happened between the Tom and Jerry of her life. She was someone both Ishaan and Meera would walk up to when they had something on their mind. Anshika knew both of them pretty well to know how volatile the equation between these two could get!

"*Accha* come, I know you have an eternal love for *mehendi*. Get some on your palms as well," Anshika said, knowing that Meera would forget things for a while if she got involved in the festivities of the wedding. Meera smiled and excitedly sat near her and started getting the beautiful designs on her hands as well.

In the extremely cold winters of Ranchi, with her eternally long hair dripping with water, she was almost shivering.

Ishaan walked towards the hall to meet Anshika and wish her. It was funny to see how inevitably awkward he was. Even though his expressions were lost and his eyes were extremely sleepy, it couldn't be denied that he looked dapper in his formal outfit. He wore a dark blue sweater over his sky blue shirt and trousers. His hair shone like silk, as always. Meera used to ruffle his hair – and as she saw him take a step near her, she remembered the best days that they had spent with each other.

Meera saw him walk towards Anshika, and it seemed as if each happy moment that they had spent was walking towards her. When a relationship goes through the ignorant phase, people often forget the cheerfulness their togetherness generated. Meera, fortunately, did not forget it; nor did Ishaan.

He tried his best to avoid looking at Meera, and just when he thought he had mastered the subtle art of not giving a fuck, his eyes were caught in the web of her dazzling smile. So then, he ended up gazing at someone he had sworn to ignore.

Wearing a yellow suit with very light make up, Meera looked gorgeous. Her golden long earrings shone through her long hair, which were still wet. Her hands chimed with the metallic bangles and the anklet peeped from below.

Looking at her red duppatta, which was flowing from her shoulder, Ishaan remembered how he always teased her saying that she had a good collection of clothes, but she was messy enough to mess that up too.

Strangely, both of them remembered everything, but nothing was required to be remembered when the strings of friendship were seemingly falling apart.

As he was lost looking at her, he noticed that Meera was neither wearing a sweater, nor was she carrying any shawl with her. Above that, she had not even dried her hair properly, and her back was all damp with it.

The mature Ishaan was back, again. *'She could have at least dried her hair before coming down. Phew, this girl is intolerable at times. Good that I am behaving in this manner. She deserves it,'* he told himself as he saw her struggling with cold. It was Ranchi, well-known for its winters, and here, this girl was trying to be a ~~superman~~ – oh, superwoman!

Ishaan simply ignored his thoughts about someone whose existence also did not matter to him. Well, at least that's what he told himself.

He then met Anshika and congratulated her most lovingly.

'*He always said he was different with different people.*' Meera was so enamoured with this warmth that she wanted to hug him, and being the typically dramatic one, she imagined having his name written on her hand with the henna. Just then, the girl putting *mehendi* on her palm said, "*Ho gaya, didi!*"

Meera gave her a smile, thanked her, and started to look around for the customs happening. She could see Anshika's face glow with happiness as she spoke to her relatives. The bride and groom would be the centre of the world for at least two days – today was Anshika's day, she thought! Meera had mocked weddings and feelings all alone, and it was really hard for her to believe that she was imagining weird stuff like writing his name on her palms.

However, as she sat down, the chill played its role well. She sneezed and sneezed. And soon after, she started having a headache too. Coughing a bit, she got up and walked up to Ishaan to ask for the keys of the room they were staying in.

"Ishaan, I need the keys of the room. I am not feeling too well. I'll go and take some rest."

She spoke confidently, but he ignored her even more confidently. She spoke with utmost hope of him replying back, but he had utmost unwillingness to. While she was bent on mending things, he was bent on breaking them.

He gave her a disgusted look, the exact one that he used as a mask to hide his care. He replied, "I don't want any *mehendi* on the keys. I will not keep it with me then."

"Good for you. I will keep the keys," she retorted.

Meera could take his tantrums, but when the competition was with hers, *thoda attitude toh banta hi hai na.*

He plastered his face with fake frustration, when in reality, it was something else. He wanted to accompany her, but being the escapist that he was acting like, forget expressing this to Meera, he did not even let those expressions express anything to himself.

"Meera, your hands are wet. I am not giving the keys to you," he declared.

He could see her eyes red with sleeplessness and her hair still wet. How he wanted to tell her that she should sleep for a while and how he wanted his other friends to take care of this girl. He also knew neither of these hopes would come true.

"What do you mean you won't give the keys to me? I can handle things myself..."

While she was talking, he started walking towards their room. Meera was clueless and angry at the same time. What kind of a person was he, she thought, as she had no other option but to follow him. Her ego was angry at her for following someone who had been questioning it for the longest time now.

He could have easily told her that he wanted to come along, but just because he had to be Ishaan, he had to act rude and arrogant, even when he wasn't. On the other hand, Meera was annoyed with herself even for being ill – typical of Ishaan and as argumentative as Meera was, typical of her as well. *Tom and Jerry was the right title for them, certainly.*

As he opened the door of their room, Meera walked inside and just went and lay down on the bed. She said, "Close the door and you can go and enjoy."

But Ishaan had sworn he would not hear a single word she said.

He walked up to her and said, "Get up!" His brain was continuously telling him not to, but he still spoke.

"Why should I?" she retorted. Ego clashes, you know!

Ishaan simply held her by her wrist and pulled her with him. Being typical of herself, she argued, "What the hell is wrong with you? You are spoiling my *mehendi*."

Ishaan took her till the chair in the room and asked her to sit. "You should have heard me at first if your *mehendi* was so precious to you," he said.

"I will not listen to you. You think I am an object—" She started again, only to be interrupted by him. He held her by her shoulders and made her sit on the chair.

"We'll discuss about equality some other day. Believe in the fact that I am a misogynist for today."

Making her sit on the chair, he brought a towel from inside the washroom and rubbed her hair to dry them off the chilled water. She looked at him as he dried her hair. Not once did he look at her, but she could look at him from the mirror. As he dried them, her golden earrings got stuck in the strands of hair.

Ishaan sat down, and ensuring she wasn't hurt, separated her hair from her earrings. Meera's eyes poured affection and that was the sole reason he didn't want to look at them. Her lips wanted to question why he still cared, but his lips would say nothing at all. There were inches in between them, but there were trillions of silent atoms distancing them from each other.

"I don't need any help," she said, but how did it matter when she knew that he wouldn't listen. He said nothing but made sure her hair were dry.

"Where is your stole?" He asked.

Now was Meera's time to be ignorant. She did not reply. Ishaan fumed for a second with the anger that was building deep inside him. He did not want to care, but he did. He did not even want to talk to her, but he did. He did not even feel like seeing her face, but he had to. Some situations, he felt, were complicated and problematic, but to pass them through with patience was his aim.

He angrily got up and got his jacket. Oh my god! A typical Bollywood scene. Didn't I mention in the disclaimer that drama was a significant hero in Meera's world?!

As he walked towards her, she said, "That's your favourite jacket and my hands have henna. It will get ruined. Do not—"

But he didn't hear. Remember he had sworn not to listen to her?

He walked a step ahead and covered her with his gray jacket – yes, the one which was his favourite. Just when he wrapped the jacket around her, there was a millisecond when they were just centimetres away from each other. For a moment, she wanted time to stop, and for a second, she prayed that this togetherness stayed forever.

Little did she know God was busy planning on the prayers she had made earlier!

Love is not obedient, is it?

Some people are emotional, some people are practical, some are expressive and some are not. But, what do you call a person who was a mixture of all of these traits?

Maybe, Ishaan?

As night covered the city as a quilt, Meera and Ishaan were left alone in the room.

While rest of their friends kept awake and enjoyed their togetherness, Meera decided to return to her room.

An hour back, when all of them sat together, Meera silently got up and mumbled, "Guys, I'll go and sleep. I feel a little tired."

And the moment she started to walk towards her room, Ishaan said, "I'll come along. I am anyway exhausted."

'She won't sleep if she was alone,' he told himself as they walked towards the room and he unlocked it.

While Meera went inside the washroom to change, Ishaan just sprawled on the bed, focussing on his phone. As she came out, he looked up at her with some frozen expressions, gave her the gray jacket and said, "Wear the jacket while sleeping. Your quilt is not sufficient enough. You'll catch a cold."

His tone was exactly like a strict maths teacher's.

"I don't need it," is all that she said as she lay down, pulling the quilt over her head.

'*I have had enough for the day,*' she told herself. The moment she closed her eyes, after fighting a few unneeded thoughts, she immediately fell off to sleep.

On the other hand, even he had not slept in these two days, had not given his brain a break, but he didn't sleep till he saw her sleeping peacefully. He pretended to be busy with his phone till the stubborn friend of his fell asleep.

As soon as he knew she was asleep, he took his jacket, and covered her ears. He saw some henna stains on the sleeves of his brand new jacket and could feel her perfume in it. And it was only after he ensured that she was warmly asleep, did he lie down and slept peacefully. *The best sleep is when you have your loved one right in front of your eyes.*

As he turned towards Meera, he could see her palms, open. It was as if they were silently asking him to hold them, to accompany them and to stay with them. And in that millisecond, he could feel the urge to hold those palms deep in his heart. For a moment, he just wanted to hold her hands, close his eyes and sleep peacefully. Love was ushering him towards Meera, but the moment love tried to do that, he immediately reminded himself that feelings were not supposed to enter between the two of them.

'*She's a lovely person, I know. But, all I feel for her is care and nothing else. I can't let myself drift away from the reality that I just don't feel for her.*' He reiterated this to himself as he closed his eyes and slept peacefully, almost ignorant of the fact that he was turning a year older the next day.

♦

Just when Ishaan opened his eyes that morning, there were no open palms. Just intertwined fingers, his and hers.

He smiled as he looked at her face. Quite unlike in Bollywood movies, Meera slept like a messy kid – her cheeks looked chubbier like a *gol gappa*, her hair were all over the face, and her quilt was only covering her feet. But the jacket had kept her warm.

Ishaan smiled at the feeling of knowing her better than she knew herself. That was his dab moment!

However, giving a tough reality check to himself, he carefully separated his fingers from hers and checked his phone, which had more than a hundred messages wishing him on his birthday. He didn't reply to any message and just got up, as if desperately trying to move out from this dream-like reality and walking into an artificial world that he was bent on creating.

He quickly got out of the room and locked it from outside as he left for breakfast, leaving Meera inside the room, sleeping peacefully.

'One-sided love is also love.'
– Zakir Khan

Meera got up an hour later, and as soon as she didn't find Ishaan, she looked at her phone. There wasn't any message from him. When she looked at the date, she smiled.

She had told herself a thousand times that she would not do anything special for his birthday. She reassured that her mind had forgotten wishing him at 12, even when she remembered the date and even when they were together, she had promised herself to not consider wishing him; and with the sun rise, she reiterated the same decision to herself.

Finding herself alone in the room, she got up and tried to open the door. But how do you think it would open, when Ishaan had locked it from outside!

Extremely annoyed with his silent attitude, Meera fumed with anger. Never did anyone behave with her the way he was behaving.

'What does he think of himself?' she thought.

'*How dare he lock me in the room?*' she added.

At that moment, her mind was saturated with argumentative thoughts. She loved him, she wanted to express it, she wanted to wish him with a hug, she wanted to make that day the most special one for him, but knowing him pretty well, she couldn't, with the fear of being ignored. One-sided love keeps self-respect on the verge of a little conversation and Meera did not want to disrespect her self-respect once again.

As she got up, annoyed and irritated by the situation, Meera called the only person she could confide in – her sister Kavya.

Eight years younger to her, Kavya was a sibling Meera could die for. In between sobs and tears, she said, "Why am I here, Kavya?"

"Di, relax! First of all, stop over-reacting on every possible thing in this world," she replied.

As temperamental as Meera was, Kavya was exactly the opposite. Where Meera panicked, Kavya relaxed; if Meera cried, her sister believed in making others cry with a smirk.

Meera narrated, "I don't know what has happened to Ishaan. He is behaving in such an unreasonable manner. Tell me one thing – is being yourself such a big crime?"

Kavya heard her quietly and replied, "I can actually console you and tell you that everything will be fine and all that bullshit. But, why should I? First, you give me some perks for listening to your ever-so-dramatic story. Then, we'll think about something."

She smirked as she knew this was the only way she could bring Meera back to normal. "You realise I am your sister, right?" Meera asked, wiping the tear drop from her moist cheeks.

"Unfortunately or fortunately – yes," Kavya replied, still laughing.

Meera kept quiet. She realised her little sister was trying to pep her up, but at that moment, she needed Ishaan.

"See di, getting miserable would neither help you nor me. Taking up your fashion blog as a priority in life can definitely help both of us, though. I get it that you love him and he is someone worth falling for, I know he's nice. But, if he doesn't want to talk, let it be."

"But, just a few months back, we were almost an inseparable part of each other's lives…" Meera tried to argue.

"So what?" Kavya immediately countered. Her voice had increased by two levels immediately. "*Arrey,* the sun changes its position in just a day; he is a human being. Till yesterday, he wanted to be your friend, and today, he doesn't feel like being one. As simple as that," Kavya continued.

"For a moment, I feel you're not my sister, but his," Meera said. A smile slowly started to make way towards her face. A cute frown followed.

"I love Ishaan bhaiya, no matter what you feel about him," Kavya replied authoritatively.

"Me too," Meera replied with a sob and a smile.

"*Ek toh,* the problem with you Cancerians is that you take everything so damn seriously. If someone says hi, you'll make a story out of it. If someone says hello, you would get till marriage and if someone like bhaiya cares for you, you'll think of what not. If you want to give him a worthy birthday gift, kick out your over-thinking. He'd be more than happy to see you carefree," Kavya said.

"Yes, right. Shut up now! Stop being Ishaan for me," Meera retorted.

As she was just about to cut the phone, Kavya said, "Di, remember… loving someone is in our hands. If they feel the same way – good, if they don't, just make things good for yourself. I don't like my sister getting vulnerable, and as much as I respect

Ishaan bhaiya, I will never forgive him for the tears I see in your eyes because of him."

Being melodramatic and somewhat Meera-ish, she replied, "No! The equation that I have with him is separate from yours. Let's not mix it up. He is the best brother you will ever have and you know this. Keep that a constant even when everything else is dynamic."

Kavya smiled at her sister. She was in class 9th, but the advices she gave were way ahead of her age. She was Meera's box of secrets – if you wanted to know anything about Meera, Kavya was the go-to person. Actually, if you also wanted to enquire anything about Ishaan, Kavya was the right person – since both of them gelled extremely well. And, that's an altogether new story. Don't worry, we'll come back to this.

Just when Meera kept the phone down, she saw a message from Ishaan.

You were sleeping and I didn't want to wake you up because you had not slept well for the last two nights. Once you are awake, give me a call and I'll open the door.

He had messaged after months and it brightened Meera's face. She almost did a little *bhangra* seeing his name on her screen. Only she knew how much had she missed those video calls, which were a routine for her.

◆

"*Bhaiya, 1 kachori, 1 samosa aur 1 litti chokha pack kar dijiye.*" He told the waiter at the restaurant they were having breakfast at.

While everyone enjoyed the sumptuous meal and were about to leave, Ishaan could not walk off without taking food for Meera. He literally tried hard to ignore the thoughts about her, but unfortunately, could not.

As the waiter turned, he added, *"Bhaiya, pyaaz aur mirchi mat daalna."*

He was like the perfect guardian for anyone – he remembered everything about Meera. And taking care of all these minute little things, he got breakfast packed for her. But when it was about giving it to her, he asked another friend to do so.

Such typical melodramatics these guys were, phew!

"Hey Kiya, you are going towards my room, no? Just take this breakfast I got for Meera."

Kiya laughed. "I can't handle kids, Ishaan. You go and feed her yourself. Anyway, kids are cranky when they get up." Kiya smirked.

Ishaan had a serious expression as he did not even hear what else his friend had to say and walked towards his room. He could get irritated and miffed on Meera, but that was just his right.

He once said, 'How could I let her cry in front of others when I know they'll make fun of her? Would I like that? Never.'

He didn't like it even today.

He always told her that he would brutally confront her with honest views so that no one else could. He did not like anyone else telling her anything – that was unacceptable to him. No matter how he behaved with her, that was his right and not anyone else's, he believed.

Not caring about anything at that moment, he walked straight inside the room, unlocking it.

♦

There was also a sense of being left alone in Ishaan today as he saw all other friends being busy in their world. They hardly cared if he was enjoying his birthday or not. For them, it was just another day where they were discussing their own banter

and plans, which he did not feel welcomed for. Sad to spend a
birthday alone, isn't it?

Weird enough, he wanted to spend time with those who
didn't care about him and wanted to run away from the person
who was ready to shower any possible happiness on him.

When he opened the door, Meera was getting ready to attend
the morning functions. While everyone, including Kiya was busy
in their fun, Meera stayed secluded. Typical of Meera. Plus,
she was on this trip only because she knew Ishaan was there.
Howsoever mad he would be at her, she knew he was the only
one who she could rely on, trust blindly. One had to understand
the silence between his words to know what he really thought.

As he entered, Meera was in front of the mirror, applying
kajal to her deeply puffy eyes.

Ishaan could see her eyes in the mirror as he entered and she
could notice his presence in the room through the same mirror.
And while both of them could feel each other, the mirror became
a witness of the crazy amount of awkwardness that flew between
the two. Their eyes had love, but their lips were sealed in silence;
their heart overflowed with joy on seeing each other, but their
expressions concealed it with ignorance towards each other.

As he entered the room, he looked at Meera – dressed in a
sky blue suit with a very heavy duppatta, she looked all ready for
the morning functions at Anshika's house. She looked extremely
pretty. She wore magenta earrings and was looking through the
bangles she wore on the henna–clad hands. He was, for once,
lost – in her innocent eyes, in her pure gaze.

'*She is a gem of a person. I really want her to do very well in
her life. I really do.*' He thought as he gazed at her.

His thoughts were interrupted abruptly when she exclaimed,
"Ouch!"

While sliding the glass bangles onto her wrist, she broke one of them and that bruised her hand. Ishaan saw this, kept the breakfast packet on the table, and walked towards her. He said, in his ever-so-wry-tone, "When you know that you had to wear these bangles, could you not check the size before buying them? You like inflicting pain on yourself."

Saying this, he also applied some moisturiser around her wrists. He then said, "Give me your bangles!"

The touch of his warm hands made Meera's heart smile. She didn't know how to react to his care and therefore, she retained a blank look. As much as she wanted to look into his eyes, he wanted to escape the gaze.

As she stared at him, Ishaan repeated, with stern looks, "Bangles?"

PS: Imagine extremely *khadoos* looks here.

He almost gave her a 'you are so hopeless' expression as he quietly held her wrist with his warm hands, took utmost care of them and slid in the bangles, patiently.

'*She looks pretty*', his heart told him and his mind immediately ignored his heart.

Within a minute, all her bangles were chirping happily on her wrist.

When a set of bangles are kept in a tight box, they tend to forget their chime. Unexpressed feelings are the same! Meera's feelings were like the bangles on her wrist – they wanted to happily chirp and tell the whole world that they were in love; while Ishaan's were stored in a dark box somewhere, if at all they existed.

Meera captured that moment in her memory – just to hide it in the treasure box of moments she had stored in her heart forever. She still loved him, after all!

That is the power of one-sided love. You are the author of the story of your life, and at the same time, you are also the author of the story from the other end – because it's about the person you love, but only from your perspective. You start each day with the hope that today, something would brew between you two, some coincidence would land you both together, something would bring you closer. And then, at the end of each day, you would hope for the next day to come with the same hopes, but that's all you have – hopes. And that is why, people who are in one-sided love are perhaps the strongest ones – when most people are unable to fight rejection, they handle it every moment and fight with the feeling of rejection to keep their self-respect alive, even when they don't feel desired. Basically, people who fall in love are lucky and those who fall in unrequited love are extremely strong.

As each bangle made the tingling sound, Meera breathed love. As she felt his touch, she felt blessed, as she could breathe the cologne he always applied, she felt mesmerised and nostalgic at the same time. As she felt his presence near her, she felt joyous and she forgot everything that troubled her.

For a second, she wanted the earth to stop revolving around the sun, she wanted every second she was spending in that moment to be like a boomerang.

She once again looked at him, and he, once again, escaped her eyes. It was just the care he had for a colleague, he said. Love, he believed, was misconceived by her.

But Meera, being Meera, was elated just by the fact that he cared for her. She gave in all her anger in that moment itself.

I told you, hopes!

She said softly, "Thank you, Ishaan. And, happy birthday."

He just put in the last set of bangles and turned towards his suitcase, taking out the coat he wanted to wear.

Somewhere, the vibe between the two of them was smoother

today – maybe, because it was his birthday. Maybe, because some distance was being reduced. Maybe –

As he pulled out a black shirt along with his black coat, Meera said, standing next to him, "The gray shirt would look better."

She knew if she stood next to him, he would never listen to her advice, so she turned and pretended to be busy with her make-up. And guess what! Ishaan broke his resolve of not listening to her. He took the gray shirt and kept it with the coat. He said, "I'll wear the shirt for lunch and then when we go for the wedding. I was thinking of putting the coat on. Do you think it would look good?"

For the first time in the last three days, he was being the way he was with her – normal. For the first time after a long time, what she thought mattered to him.

Meera nodded and smiled softly. She immediately wanted to ask, 'Let's go out for lunch?' but she didn't.

She rather asked, "Where's everyone else, Ishaan?"

"They are all going to Anshika's place; after which, they plan to go out for shopping in the market nearby. Kiya was saying they'll then visit the parlour to get ready for the evening," he replied, rather wryly.

Meera could see the potential this conversation had. (If I forgot, one-sided love makes you a pro at stalking the other person's mind as well! (Wink))

She asked, "And, they will return only by evening, right?"

He nodded, looking in his phone. He was missing home, she could see.

"Ishaan – umm – actually..."

"What?" He looked up.

"I was thinking that going alone to Anshika's place for lunch isn't such a great idea. They would have many relatives already;

we'll feel a bit out of place without our friends. And, I don't want to behave goodie-good right now. So, I was wondering if we can have lunch in some nearby restaurant?"

Very smart! Yes, she was a kid because she wanted to see everyone happy, despite the way they behaved with her. Yes, she was a kid, because she felt like standing by him just because it was his birthday. Yes, she was a kid because a kid was as innocent as she was – thinking she was doing well, but ended up getting scolded by everyone who was plagued by the practical world. Maturity, they called it. Pretence, she called it.

Ishaan said, "Let's see. First, at least have breakfast."

Meera smiled as she saw the breakfast packet kept on the table. She knew the day would be a happy one. At least, she *hoped* so.

'Saath khane se pyaar badhta hai.'

"I am very hungry, Ishaan. I need food," Meera declared as both of them lay down in two diametrically opposite corners of the bed.

Ishaan looked at his watch. It was 2 p.m. already. He called his friends to ask if they wanted to take lunch. He wasn't surprised, neither was he too happy knowing the fact that everyone else had already taken lunch.

He then said, "Where do you want to go?"

"Anywhere," she replied casually, looking in her phone. These two had a habit of escaping by turning to their phones.

"What sort of an answer is that?" he mumbled.

This time she ignored it; with a smirk, of course. "Nothing has changed," he added as he looked in his phone, looking for nearby restaurants.

"Nothing would," she mumbled.

For a millisecond, both of them remembered the good times

when Meera would always be both – unconditionally clueless and unimaginably argumentative. He fumed a bit, partially because she was responsible to take him to the good-old times, which he wanted to erase from his memory and partially because he reiterated to himself that she still needed to grow up.

After his fuming was done with, Ishaan said, "Kaveri is a good restaurant – it has sweets. *Wahan chalien?*"

Meera smiled as she heard sweets. It was his favourite and having shared a table with him multiple times now, it was her favourite too. She nodded as she got up to leave.

Meera was too lazy to change her suit, which by the way was sleeveless and backless. She asked, like a little kid would, "You think I would need a swea..."

Even before she could complete her sentence, he replied, "Obviously! You will not go outside in a half sleeve dress. Wear the gray jacket." He probably knew she would argue on something as vague as this and hence, without saying anything, he picked up his jacket and gave it to her.

"I would look like a joker if I wear a gray jacket over my well-designed *kurti*," she argued.

This time, even Meera knew that the argument was vague, but she still wanted to argue. Habits! As if there was a competition between the two of them – who could be more unreasonable.

Ishaan knew she could be unreasonable to the power of infinity and therefore, he simply left the room, mumbling, "Like, if you don't wear the jacket, you would look like Cinderella. Come only if you have the jacket on. Otherwise, I'll go alone!"

"You are as stubborn as you always were," she mumbled as she wore the jacket.

"Super *khadoos*. Nothing has changed." She added angrily as she locked the room and walked by his side.

♦

Kaveri was one of the most decent places Ishaan and Meera could find nearby. As they walked together towards the restaurant, which was at a walking distance from the marriage venue, Ishaan walked ten steps either ahead of her or behind her. *Kya kar sakte hain* – he was being himself; he was escaping her. Everyone has a right to be their own selves, *haina?*

Observing this, Meera stopped when he was rushing ahead. As she stood there and saw him walking alone, she realised she couldn't see him alone.

'No *matter if he feels for me or not, being a friend, how could I let his birthday be? I have to make it special,*' she told herself and quickly messaged the others.

> Let's celebrate Ishaan's birthday. See if you all can come by 3.30 p.m.

Meanwhile, he kept walking. He realised that she wasn't following, but he didn't stop because he never looked back. Ishaan had a habit of walking ahead – be it in the most crowded metro or the airport, he would never look back and wait for her, while she would always turn to see if he was there or not. For Ishaan, this was growing up and for Meera, if this was about growing up, she was happy being a kid.

He turned only after reaching a considerable distance and called her up, saying, "Walk straight and you'll find me." And without listening to what she had to say, he kept the phone.

Meera did not pay heed to the tone in which he had spoken to her; rather she excitedly asked Google for the best cake shops around, just to find that she did not have Swiggy or Zomato to deliver cakes in an hour at Lalpur Chowk, Ranchi.

Figuring out alternatives, while her brain was running at full speed, she reached in front of the restaurant, where he stood, waiting for her, looking extremely irritated by her speed.

"Thank god, you arrived," he said, walking ahead.

Meera replied, "You should actually thank god – not everyone gets to have lunch with me!" She replied as she walked down the stairs to reach the restaurant.

She took a seat and he sat right opposite, giving her completely blank expressions, escaping even looking at her.

Secretly, he missed the childish charm in her voice too, but as I was telling you, these guys had promised each other to not express – ever.

The waiter brought the menu, and Ishaan pointed it towards her, even when he knew that she couldn't complete anything alone. Forget one big *thali*, Meera needed his help to finish the meagre amount of white sauce pasta that they served in their office canteen. Every time they went out together, she would order and he would finish her order.

In that moment, he got a major throwback to the times when he always called himself her garbage bin. He knew that as soon as the waiter turned, Meera would look at him and ask him to order. And, his thoughts didn't need to wait much to become reality.

As soon as the waiter turned, Meera said, "Ishaan, you decide and order something for me as well."

He smiled a bit. But, *na na* – he couldn't keep that smile for long. He quickly replaced it with the serious look he had mastered for her. The typical Ishaan-look, remember? He looked at the menu with his almond-shaped eyes, asking her, "Let's order one thali?"

Of course! What was better than having lunch with him on his birthday, from the same thali? *Saath khaane se toh pyaar badhta hai na*!

But, painting that excitement with an expression of indifference, she said, "Umm, if that's what we have to do, I am fine with it."

◆

While he was busy fiddling with his mobile, Meera quickly got up and walked till the counter of sweets. He saw her walk away and once he checked she was around, he didn't care.

Meera asked the guy at the counter to pack one kilo of *moong dal halwa*. She requested him to get her a plate and some candles. If you are wondering what this girl was up to, Meera was trying to make a cake from that halwa. She took the halwa and pressed it tightly inside the box with the help of a spoon. She then turned it over on a decorative plate that she had covered with foil and lo, she got her base made.

Ishaan turned around and saw her talking to the shopkeeper. '*God save the poor shopkeeper*,' he told himself as he saw Meera excitedly instructing him to get more dry fruits and decorative. She generally spoke with sugar coating and it was difficult to say no to her. He knew she could go out of the way to make anyone feel special and he realised he was already pretty special for her. He knew she was up to something for sure as he turned back to his phone.

Meera quickly made a smiley on the base of the cake with dry fruits and then, as she was done, she asked the shopkeeper to pack the cake in a box. She quickly paid and came back to the table, where the thali was waiting, and Ishaan had not taken a single bite.

She sat and as she tore the first bite from the plate, she said, "It isn't that hot."

He mumbled, "You realise that I can, but the chapatti can't wait for her highness to come back, madam."

She smiled at his sense of humour and looked at him with her typical sheepish smile. For a change, Ishaan smiled back. As they looked at each other, the moment was worth being clicked with food waiting for them and they being lost in each other's eyes. How often does it happen that you don't pay heed to the delicious food that is kept for you? Rare, isn't it?

In the past month, they had not even had tea together. Those who were like the strings of infinity entangled in one another were now like the broken threads distanced by feelings.

And just when he realised he had been distracted, Ishaan said, tearing a piece of chapatti, "Let's have lunch and go back to the venue. I have to get ready too."

Meera smiled and chewed the *butter naan*. While eating, Ishaan made sure she had her lunch properly. He said, "Try this, this is good."

For once, Meera told god to make the two of them together forever. Only she knew how much she prayed for him to be near her. She took a bite and smiled.

Some of the most beautiful moments are hidden in the shortest memories, maybe.

'Meera cares for him; she's such a kid.'

Walking back to the hotel room, Meera held the cake and Ishaan knew exactly what she was up to. Looking at her, he fumed. He did not like people doing anything special for him. He felt Meera was trying to be an intruder in his life. I am sure, God must be thinking of aliens when Ishaan was born.

While normal people reacted happily to surprises, and got joyous when they saw people care for them, Ishaan reacted unhappily to everything that made him feel special. Strangely, since morning, he was missing home on his birthday, and now, when someone was finally trying to make his day special, he wasn't happy with that as well.

Many times, people say, don't give importance to boys; they can't handle it. I really feel that this man validated this comment time and again. While he could care for her, when she cared for him – he just couldn't accept the fact. That's also a problem with people who care a lot for others – they stop pampering themselves and that, my friend, is pretty dangerous.

As he again walked ten steps ahead, Meera called, "Ishaan!" She didn't expect him to turn to her, but he loved playing with her expectations, always.

He turned.

What if the distance between their hearts could not be reduced, at least the steps between them could. Meera took those ten steps to minimize the distance between them and as she stood exactly in front of him, she said, "I am sorry. I know you are already annoyed with everyone else and their tantrums. Whatever trip is left, I promise there wouldn't be a single second where you'll feel burdened with me being around."

She smiled and this time, she walked ten steps ahead.

He had no expressions – his face was devoid of any smile, any smirk. What had happened to him, even he didn't know. An hour ago, he was happily having lunch with her, enjoying the day, and just when she thought she would make him feel special, his expressions got sombre. Weirdo, he was. At times, I really quip, '*why do we have to make life complicated when it is served simply and then complain that it's complicated?*'

◆

Once back at the room, Meera arranged for everything; she tried decorating the room with whatever little time that she had. She had less time and lesser resources, but the energy and zeal with which she worked was incomparable. While the rest of their friends decided to arrive as guests, Meera kept Ishaan away to peacefully make all the efforts to make his day special for him.

For the next thirty minutes, she was devotedly involved in making the room look happening and once she had made it look colourful and hep, she asked their friends to come. She excitedly opened the door to get Ishaan near her, when she saw him walking towards the room with Kiya – hand in hand. As they entered hand in hand, Meera stood in one corner, carrying a vivacious smile.

Yes, she was upset, but her smile was genuine. When she saw him smile, how could she not be happy? Well done, Meera! She had already reached a 'no expectation stage'. Impressive!

And as dramatic as it might sound, she just prayed that all his dreams came true in the next year. Standing in the same corner, Meera saw him cut the cake and smiled at his smile. But, when he cut six pieces and fed everyone with his hands, the seventh piece was left unattended – with the assumption that Meera was unimportant enough and she would anyway take it herself.

Did he realise that she had put in every effort she could to make his day happier? Did he realise that the cake he had so easily distributed to all others who didn't give a damn about him was made by someone who loved him unconditionally? Perhaps, that is why, always keep people in the place they deserve; the moment they start becoming your life, life takes a back seat.

He didn't even look at Meera, and Meera, who constantly looked at him, expected just one smile – if not of appreciation, at least of acknowledgment, which she knew in that moment that she would never get from the person she loved.

One-sided love, maybe.

'Expectations are the root cause of frustration.' Poor Shakespeare has been saying this since ages, but *hum samjhein tab na*. Meera, however, did not let that smile vanish from her face till she left the room and ran outside, when she was unable to control the tears that had accumulated inside her eyes.

While she could not wipe the thoughts that troubled her, she immediately wiped the tears from her face. She stood on the road, looking at the cars and rickshaws passing by, questioning herself.

'Why? Why am I the scapegoat every time? Did he not see

that I was the one making all the arrangements and I did not even have a problem with everyone else saying that they did it, but couldn't he come and tell me that I was important to him? Why am I the stupid kid who is just sidelined every time? It feels as if I am just a burden for him and to everyone here – why! The fashion blogger, Meera Tiwari – what the fuck am I doing to myself?'

Posing all these questions to destiny, she kept wiping the tears that her eyes were filled with.

Meera walked towards the main road and just stood at the entrance of the hotel, blank and helpless. There were thousands of thoughts revolving in her mind. Her brain wanted to hate him, her senses sensed that she was being a fool – but, even when logic suggested that he wasn't correct, her heart simply refused to believe this fact. She simply kept reiterating to herself, *'It's his birthday. No matter what, you will not spoil it, Meera.'* Thinking so, she wiped all her tears and grudges away.

While she was fighting with her emotions and herself, Ishaan found an off-white sweatshirt with orange and blue stripes kept in his suitcase. It simply read, 'HAPPY BIRTHDAY, ISHAAN.'

From the writing, he knew it was Meera, and because it was her present, he did not have to acknowledge it, he knew. He did not even look at it properly and kept it inside. But, for a second, even he questioned himself, *'Why is this girl doing all this to herself? I very well know that no one else bothered about the cake, and she did. No one else had the time to come and wish me, but she did. How do I tell her I felt good when she made the day so special. How do I tell her that I wanted to thank her? But, if I would have gone in front of her, I would have expressed more than what I should have. I am fine the way I am, why can't she accept this? Why does she want me to be happy – even when she is not?'*

There were two minds working at the same time, questioning themselves for what they were doing – breaking piece by piece, separating thread by thread. It was easier to understand Meera's perspective – she loved him and she was hurt because he ignored her. But, it was extremely difficult to understand Ishaan – he didn't know if he loved her or not, but he knew he had to keep himself away from her. He obviously did not have the dramatic reasons and melodrama in his life, but yet, there was something, somewhere.

Together?

It was already 5:30 p.m. and they had to reach the wedding venue by 7. Except Meera, all the girls were in the parlour, getting ready for the wedding. Meera stayed back in the room and just got busy with some blog of hers.

Typical of her – whenever emotions were too complicated for her to handle, she turned to her work, with five-fold effort. She was writing down something in her little blue diary when Ishaan looked at her.

She was sitting cross-legged on the bed, with her hair flowing freely and her eyes looking as worried as ever. But, her face had a charm, the charm he knew she had when she was working on her blog. Even when she was tired of emotions, her brain ran at full speed, and he, for a second, prayed that this charm stayed there forever.

'*She's meant to achieve the greatest dreams she has seen and nothing can deviate her from her focus. She deserves the best in this field. I get inspired by her motivation to work. Hats off to this girl for pulling everything off so easily!*' He thought as he kept staring at her. He had always appreciated and taken inspiration from the workaholic in her.

He then said, softly, "Meera, do you want to get ready? I can go outside."

"You get ready first. I'll go outside and write there," she replied politely, took her notebook and left. Ishaan quickly changed and wore the shirt Meera had suggested.

'*Aaja!*' he said softly, once he was done.

As Meera looked up, she felt like she would lose her heart once again to the same man. He looked handsome in the gray shirt, black jeans and his stubble. However, his hair was as simple as he always kept them. Meera so wanted to ruffle them, but she remembered she had been humiliated a few hours back and hence, she quietly entered and started to look for her clothes.

Ishaan looked in the mirror and was trying to put his tie, unable to tie it. *Bollywood scenes do happen in real life. This one did as well.* He asked, "Do you know how to tie a tie?"

Meera looked up at him and smiled. She replied, "Yes, that's all I learnt in college."

Saying so, she walked towards him and opened a tutorial on how to tie a tie on YouTube. She followed the instructions and tied his black tie. For once, Ishaan's mind directed him to take a step back from her because the distance between them was reducing, which he couldn't afford, but at that moment, something magical just stopped him from doing anything that reduced the distance between them.

While following the instructions in the video, Meera did not realise that she was inches away from him. As she looked up at his face, their eyes had each other's reflection in them and their unsaid words were readable in those eyes. Ishaan simply admired her innocence; he could see honesty and charm that expressed all her feelings.

While he read her feelings in her eyes, she was lost in his, trying to guess what his reason for being rude could be.

The next minute, Meera said, "Such blank expressions and plain hair just ruin the charm of this suit."

Ishaan replied, without using his brain, "Expressions are such since birth, but I think hair—"

He was just about to complete his sentence, when Meera ruffled his hair through her fingers and said, "Now you look perfect!" She winked; he smiled. The room instantly had a glitter of happiness, which had gone missing since afternoon. This was just like Meera's face, which was devoid of all expressions a few minutes ago, but was glimmering with the spark of love now.

He said, while putting his wallet into his pocket, "Is there anything you want to carry to the garden? We'll keep the rest of the luggage inside the car, since we directly leave for the airport in the morning."

Meera was busy matching her dress with jewellery she had brought and hence, she replied casually, "I've already kept everything inside my suitcase. I don't need anything outside."

"What are you wearing for the evening?" he asked, knowing she would be shivering outside.

"Clothes," she replied, with a mean smile.

He walked near her and looking at her dress, he said, "You are a wearing a backless top and you say, you won't need anything."

"Yes. And that's none of your business. I obediently heard what you said in the morning, but don't expect that now. I am not going to wear any jacket over this."

Ishaan walked a step ahead and explained, "You understand the difference in wearing a jacket and keeping one?"

Meera replied with a 'whatever' expression and said, "I need to change. Go out."

♦

In flat fifteen minutes, she was ready in her sky blue lehenga, teamed with a golden backless blouse. The lehenga had a texture of cotton and the dupatta looked elegant, but was quite heavy. Meera told herself, "Meera Tiwari looks pretty. This blend of cotton works well. Nice design, Meera."

Yes, it was her design and it looked lovely on her. As she kept looking at her dress, Ishaan knocked, "Are we done, madam?"

She smiled and opened the door. Ishaan entered without even looking at her and said, "Kiya had called. They are coming in a cab. Is your luggage packed?"

"Yes, except a few things, for which I did not have any space in my suitcase," she replied, with a puppy face.

"Give all of that to me!"

Saying so, he arranged all her bangles, her earrings and her cosmetics in a box and kept it inside his suitcase, leaving a bracelet on the table, looking at which, Meera said, "You missed keeping this. Wait! This isn't mine."

"Someone was shouting over the phone for the four days I was in Hyderabad that she wanted a bracelet. So I got it. See if you want to wear it, or I'll keep it inside with the rest of your jewellery."

Meera almost jumped with excitement. Yes, she had repeatedly told him to get her a pearl bracelet when he was in Hyderabad for a client meeting. She just remembered those days when they spoke for hours, days and weeks continuously. She knew every detail of his life even when he was millions of kilometres away. Unlike today, when she didn't know a single thing, even when he was steps away.

She smiled and replied, "This is beautiful. Help me put this on my wrist."

Ishaan smiled and helped her wear it. It was a trendy bracelet with pearls and dolphins and it looked delicate on her petite wrist. Meera smiled and looked at him and once again, there was glitter, till they started walking out with their luggage.

Rest of their friends were already waiting in the cab. And as Ishaan kept their bags in the cab, Kiya said, "Ishaan, I don't think there would be sufficient place for the two of you. Plus, sitting too tight would just ruin our sarees. Maybe, one of us could just adjust with Anshika's relatives. I spoke to them; they are starting in a bit as well."

Ishaan did not even take a minute and said, "Meera can go with them."

Meera looked at him and then just went blank for a second. He said, "Come, I'll—"

She interrupted, "If I have to go with strangers, I might as well just go and talk to them myself. You guys continue."

Saying so, she turned and walked away. Being Meera, she would never walk to someone and ask them to accommodate her, and hence, she simply booked a cab.

He very well knew how egoistic she was. Well, now this was what was not considered a mature idea – in Ranchi, at 7 p.m., she had to go till the outskirts of the city and she had taken a cab to go alone.

Meera kept thinking why she was always the first choice that he wanted to eliminate from his life.

♦

While everyone else enjoyed their gala time in the other cab, Ishaan called Meera. Her phone was not reachable.

'Damn, why is the bloody phone not reachable? She would

never go and tell someone that she has to tag along with them. How would she show off her princess-like ambience otherwise? I'm so sure she took a cab.'

As they covered their distances separately, Meera's cab driver said, "Madam, are you a Dhoni fan?"

Sceptical and sad, she said, "Hmm."

"*Dhoni bhaiya ka purana ghar aaega abhi raste me. Humare Ranchi ki saan hai Dhoni bhaiya,*" he said proudly in his accent.

Meera smiled, wiping a tear from her right eye. She looked at the bracelet and thought, how come he cared, yet he didn't. How could she believe that whatever was between them was nothing when she knew there was something evidently present?

She smiled at the driver as he drove swiftly through the dark roads. For once, Meera was scared because the roads were isolated. Deep inside, she was scared. She asked, "*Bhaiya, kitni der aur hai?*"

She tried reaching Google Maps, but her network connections were bleak. In between her despair of being abandoned, she got goose bumps on the fact that her phone had zero network.

'*Wow, no network again. I need a new phone the moment I get back,*' she told herself.

However, the driver was a genuine person. He replied, "Five minutes, madam!"

Meera told him they might have to look around for the venue, to which the cab driver replied, "*Madam, mehman ho aap humare. Jimmedari hai ki aapko sahi pahucha dein.* I will make sure a guest to our city finds her destination."

Meera smiled, and immediately remembered the 'Incredible India' ads. She was happy that those ads were not fictitious and existed in reality as well. She felt proud of her country and that drove her mind apart from the pain that it was going through.

On the other hand, while Ishaan continuously tried Meera's

phone, he asked Kiya, "Do you have anyone's number in Anhsika's family, who is at the marriage garden?"

Kiya replied, "Nope. I am not a directory, am I?"

While she said so, one of their friends asked the driver to stop the car. He said, "We need an envelope to put the cash in. I'll go and get it. We are still in the city."

Ishaan replied impulsively, "We can't. Meera's phone is not reachable."

"So? She can manage things. Stop being her guardian," his friend replied as he got off the cab.

Ishaan fumed as they stopped for the envelope. '*I shouldn't have left her alone. I knew she is stubborn. Damn, why did I leave her? In trying to escape her company, I ended up risking her safety. Is escaping love so important that I could afford losing her in that?* ' He cursed and questioned himself as he helplessly sat in the car.

◆

While they were still in the city, making all possible delays, Meera reached the marriage garden and met Anshika's mom. Aunty asked, "Where are your friends?"

Meera smiled and replied, "They are just on their way, aunty."

I must say, she was a genius at hiding her emotions. Or perhaps, she had become one on this trip. Experience is a good teacher.

Meera checked her phone, and there was no network. So she made her way at the corner of the venue, and while everyone was happily enjoying the ambience of festivities, she desperately tried to focus on Subway Surfers. I told you, that was her escape. While she sat and saw relatives and friends enter, she adorned an artificial smile on her face.

The fact that he had suggested her to go away was something that pinched her. And as she stared at the screen of the mobile phone, a tear drop accumulated in her eyes and fell on the screen. *She lost the game which she was winning.*

Just then, Ishaan ran through the door of the garden, leaving their luggage, his friends and even his ego behind and rushed towards the banquet hall, looking around for her – everywhere. He felt Meera wasn't dependable when it came to taking care of herself. Although, she was always a perfectionist when it came to taking responsibilities and handling work pressure, but when it came to herself, she messed things up, he knew.

Ishaan walked past everyone, only wanting to see Meera. He had never been this panic-stricken earlier. '*She would take a bundle of wool, open it, sort it and then jumble it again. Meera can dramatise any and every situation,*' he thought.

She saw him from inside the hall. For a second, her heart smiled, then her ego returned and she continued playing her game in her phone.

While he looked around, hassled and troubled, he entered the banquet and scanned it to find her sitting on the last chair. He couldn't express how relaxed he was when he saw her – safe and sound. He kept looking at her in the hope that she would look up and he would call her outside, but now was her time to take revenge.

He walked towards her; she deliberately kept playing. In fact, the focus she had in her phone doubled immediately. Even when he came and stood by her side, expecting her to get up, she didn't.

"Your phone—" He tried to start a conversation, looking at the anger in her brightly-sparkling eyes.

Meera got up angrily and walked outside the banquet hall. She wanted to go away from the glitter into darkness and hence walked towards a comparatively isolated side of the marriage garden. The place where the caterers kept the extra utensils – just there.

Ishaan had expected this and he very well understood her reaction. He somehow always sensed whenever Meera was upset.

He walked behind her. For a change, he was following her.

"Meera!"

Meera did not stop and kept walking till she sat on the farthest corner of the garden. Ishaan followed and made a place to sit down near her.

Wearing a pretty expensive, self-designed lehenga, Meera had found a brilliant way of ruining it, he thought. She just sat down on dusty chairs and didn't speak a single word. Ishaan had to accompany her silence and he did – silently, as always.

No one spoke for the next five minutes. He knew her anger was volatile and as much as his was passive, hers was volcanic. Either she bashed the anger out or when, at times, she did not speak, the volcano would be burning inside her and would burst emotionally.

He knew she needed him and the silence to calm her down. For once, he thought, '*Let her handle it herself. She needs to grow up and stop being dependent on me.*'

But, the next moment his heart rejected this idea. '*If you have put her here, it's your duty to take her out as well.*'

As they sat quietly, Ishaan remembered those times when Meera would be immensely irritated by whatever was happening in the office and would enter the cab, cribbing and angry. He would irritate her more so that all her anger vented out till they reached Huda City Centre Metro station and she could focus on her blog.

He smiled noticing how nothing had changed, even when

everything actually had, he tried initiating a conversation, ignoring his brain, which continuously asked him not to.

"Look—"

"Leave me alone and go! Just like you did an hour back and just like you will always do," she said, sternly. Her eyes sparkled, not with any eye shadow or glitter, but with anger, which was burning her inside out.

It wasn't an easy day for him today, he knew simply by looking into her eyes. To calm her down, he peacefully placed his hand over hers and replied, "Meera, listen to me!"

Meera slipped her hands from his and replied, "What if I don't want to?"

Ishaan looked at her, peacefully. And left it to silence. He knew she would say something.

"Am I a throw bag – when you wish, we talk, when you wish, we don't?"

Ishaan said, "I just thought you wouldn't be comfortable with others—"

Meera brought her palm in front of his eyes and signalled him to shut up. After a minute, she looked away, while he kept quiet. His mind was constantly telling him to simply stay away from her, but right now, he followed his heart.

He held her hand again and sat on the ground in front of her, looking straight into her eyes. "Meera, I am sorry."

"Sorry. Wow. Just get one word for everything wrong you do. If I make a mistake, it becomes a blunder that a kid is doing, but what about you? You were supposed to be mature. Is this the maturity that you boast about, Ishaan?"

Saying so, Meera angrily took her hands away and got up. She just turned to walk away from him.

"Listen to me, once." Ishaan tried his best to stop her.

"Why? Do you listen to me when I had things to clarify? Can I know what I have done to deserve the attitude you have been showing towards me since all these months? I have the right to know why I'm being dealt with like I am just no one in your life? You realise that this questions me, my self-confidence and my pride on myself…"

He tried to speak in between, but was bluntly cut, again.

"I am not done," she said angrily and continued, "So, you know what? I don't give a fuck about others – *aap jaante ho mujhe farak nahi padta*. But, when it comes to you, my whole world gets affected. It shouldn't, I know, and I don't know why it does. It's your birthday, and trust me, I made all the possible efforts to not have this conversation that we are having today. But no, you would want us to fight like cats and dogs even today…"

As she was speaking angrily, he just took a step ahead and gave her a tight hug. For a second, everything was glittery in that dark night. Meera just felt as if the whole world was smiling at her and she was in the safest embrace that she could ever be. On the other hand, Ishaan knew nothing else but the fact that she needed to be calmed down. She had waited for this trip to Ranchi, he knew; and he had intentionally and unintentionally spoilt it, he knew that too.

He had never seen her so angry and miserable. As he wrapped his arms around her, he could feel her gushing heartbeats. He could sense the turmoil in her heart. He just locked his arms around her and tightened the grip, pulling her closer to himself. He did not want that moment to go. He wanted it to stay forever. He closed his eyes, wishing for brightness for her.

On the other hand, Meera felt magical. His embrace was blissful for her – she once again wanted time to stop there and pause forever. As he hugged her, she hid her emotions, her feelings, her problems, and her anger in him. The warmth that she could feel was something she couldn't express – it was beyond real, it was eternal.

As she stayed in his embrace, her anger evaporated and the pain she had buried in her heart was set free the moment he touched her. His company was the world to her. This time too, it was evident.

Imagine if all relationships could be so simple that one hug could sort everything out? Here, it could, but the two people involved just didn't like things to be sorted and simple.

She said, "And, this is not fair. You can't stop me from complaining."

"That no one has the guts to, madam," he replied.

Meera wiped a tear and smiled. She started walking back towards the venue, when Ishaan said, "Ever looked at your anger?"

"Yes, it's a little less passively volatile than yours," she retorted.

As he saw the glitter in her eyes, he thought, *'I know what we have between us is much beyond what I want it to be. I know you like me, but you love your blog. How could I even think of distracting you from the ultimate aim of your life? I am just afraid of your reaction when this day ends, Meera. I don't know how to handle you when you will get to know the reality.'*

Reality was that he didn't feel for her the way she did. At least that's what he told us, right?

As they walked, Ishaan noticed that the safety pin tying her heavy dupatta was unpinned.

'A fashion blogger cannot have a messy dupatta,' he thought.

And fighting the guidelines that his ignorant brain was giving, he said, "Pin the dupatta!"

Meera looked at it and said, "It has a very heavy border.

Putting the pin for the first time in itself was a task. I can't do it again. Let it be!"

"You are a fashion blogger," he said, sternly.

Looking at his expression, she quickly turned and tried pinning the dupatta to her blouse. But wasn't able to. Turning back at that angle, and pinning that heavy dupatta without piercing her skin seemed like a task.

"Give that pin to me," he said, looking at the pin. "Only if you don't have a problem," he quickly added.

'*Why would I have a problem?*' she thought, smiled sheepishly and nodded.

She handed the safety pin to him and saw him diligently struggling. She just saw him from the corner of her eyes and mumbled, "Thank you, Ishaan."

Ishaan just looked at her and smiled. '*This smile of yours is priceless. But, the one that would be after seeing your fashion blog do extremely well would be so much brighter.*'

He said, "You are getting cold. I have my jacket inside the bag. You can change after some time."

Meera smiled and after the dress was all set, they both walked towards the marriage hall. They were together for the rest of the night; even till the marriage ceremonies began. With him, the starters tasted better, the drinks were yummier, the food more sumptuous.

'Okay, let's just switch off the button of emotions, Meera.'

As the night passed, the chilling air started to result in back to back sneezes for Meera. Noticing that, she got up and told Ishaan, "I need to change. You got my jacket, right?"

"Yes, I have my jacket in my bag," he replied sitting quietly, pretty tired.

"Where are the bags? I need my jeans as well," she said, almost ordering. It was as if Meera's original self was back. And unfortunately, Ishaan's original self too started coming back.

He replied, "Go and figure that out yourself."

At midnight, after a day full of emotional ups and downs, she no longer wanted to tolerate his 'figure-it-out-yourself' theory. She simply got up and started to move towards the rooms. By that time, only a few relatives from Anshika's family stayed awake for the wedding rituals and therefore, most of the rooms were already occupied with everyone sleeping.

'Now, she'll go alone and then enter the wrong room,' he told himself.

He walked towards her and said, "Room number 114. Here, take the keys!"

Minimalistic dialogues were something he loved. If there was an energy saving award by not speaking, our Ishaan would get two, or may be three.

Yet again, the original Ishaan was back. He just loved being rude, even when his heart desperately wanted him to be good.

"*Akdu,*" she mumbled.

"Do not even think of wearing that turquoise jacket of yours; it isn't warm enough. Wear the gray one that I have kept for you."

Meera heard him and smiled. Secretly, she had wished when he was keeping that jacket inside that he tells her to wear it. Now that it had actually happened, she felt elated. '*Now I would never blame Bollywood for setting wrong expectations,*' she thought.

She removed all her jewellery and literally dumped it inside his bag. Quickly, she changed into a pair of jeans and wore his jacket over her blouse.

As she wore the jacket, she could feel him and his cologne. That relaxed her. She could live with that feeling forever, she knew.

Dumping the lehenga in his purple bag pack, Meera was about to close the door, when she just took a step back and checked her bag for the Vicks tablets that she had kept in the bag for him. Ishaan had a sore throat since the last two days and knowing that he would never think of taking care of himself, she knew she had to.

As she walked outside the room, she took his hand and placed the cough droplets in his hands, saying, "Have some hot coffee as well."

The person for whom care was a burden would definitely not react positively to such a gesture, right?

Wrong. He admired the care that she had for him. But yes, at the same time, he also wondered why she cared for him the way she did. She knew what colour shirts he had, she knew when he wasn't fine, she knew when he felt bad, she knew when he wanted to be carefree and keep the burden of being silent aside. She perhaps knew him too well, but he always felt she knew only what he said. How silly of him!

As they walked in the dimly lit light of the corridor, Ishaan asked, "This is warm enough, right?"

Meera nodded and smiled a bit. As they walked, for her, the distance was reducing, while for him, his brain was constantly asking him to take a step away from her. Why, even he didn't know.

Upon reaching the *mandap*, where the ceremony had to take place, they sat next to each other but thought of two completely different scenarios.

Meera, being the fantasy-dreamer, thought of the next scene being that of Ishaan and her sitting there and taking the seven vows. For a minute, her fashion blog, her dreams and aspirations and the fact that she wanted to sit on her fashion house's CEO's chair – everything took a back seat because at that point of time, all she wanted was what she was imagining. All her wishes had come down to one word – Ishaan.

On the other hand, the brain that sat next to her was aware of what was going on in her mind. For him, the fashion blog was the reason he started talking to her, her dreams were the reason he felt she was worthy of befriending. The aspirations that she had earlier was the reason he loved her. If that did not exist anymore, Meera would not exist for herself, he knew. Today, his love was important to her, he agreed. But, in the longer run, never would she be able to accept a life which was monotonous and he knew what she was imagining was drifting her away from the dreams that she had seen. Being a best friend, how could he let love enter between Meera and her dreams. Even when his heart wanted to, he would not let that happen.

Looking at her from the corner of his eyes, he thought, '*Meera Tiwari – the name suits with the tag of a fashion icon. How can anything or anyone even think of entering her world of ambitions?*

'*Plus, she is the same girl who ran away from commitment. Today, it's just that she is attracted towards these feelings. But she might, yet again, forget what commitment is when it comes to her dreams. Meera needs to realise what her dreams are for her.*

'*She is just a kid right now, but I am twenty-six. I have to drift her away from me, so that the place that I have taken in her life is replaced rightfully by her dreams. Plus, I don't feel the same way for her – yes, I don't… If she misinterpreted care as love, that is not my problem, right?*'

The day had ended. The way he was with her was a dream she had always seen and which came true as well, but the pledge he had taken was now to shatter those dreams. It wasn't any dramatic sacrifice that he wanted to make. You know Ishaan was not dramatic. That was Meera's department.

The problem with him was that he thought he didn't like Meera. And he had reasons to believe he perhaps just cared for her. His care was the reason she misunderstood the feelings between them as love, which did not exist. Or even if it did, he didn't want to accept it.

But, when Meera was someone who would express without any second thoughts, the person in front of her had to take that path, maybe for himself, maybe for her, maybe for the betterment of her dreams. Correct or incorrect, Ishaan had decided what he had to do. And like always, he had his reasons to believe that he was right.

He didn't have to work that hard – he just needed to turn off all the emotions and switch to his rude self. He always said, "When I tend to get rude, there are no limits."

It was time that he proved himself right. *'If she won't see me for ten days, she'll forget me,'* he told himself. *'Anyway, whatever she has is a mere crush. It will subside, I am sure.'*

That was *his* definition of Meera's love. The best part was that he defined her definition of love because, of course, she was a kid; how could she define things for herself, right?

So, well – the decision was taken, for the two of them.

Happy life ahead?

As beautifully as the moon made way for the sun, the most beautiful day of Meera's life came to a serene end, with Anshika's smile being the showstopper for the day. That moment when all the rituals are finally completed and finally you know, *he is the one* – it was that smile.

Meera looked at Anshika and told Ishaan, "That smile on her face is just priceless. *Haina?*"

Ishaan first looked at Anshika, smiling at her happiness; he then looked at Meera – who was smiling as generously as she could. For a moment, he felt proud to know a girl like Meera – she was happy for everyone, was sharing the burden of sadness whenever it became difficult for her friends to handle it alone, she was there – always; no matter if that care was reciprocated or not! If he had ever understood the word 'selfless', it was when he met her, and her smile had proven it yet again.

He mumbled looking blankly at her, "Yes, when the smiles have a spark of innocence, they are the most beautiful."

They all started packing up to leave for the airport.

One of his friends asked him, "Ishaan, just lend me your gray jacket. My coat is not very comfortable for a journey..." Pausing for a moment, his friend said, "Wait, how are you wearing the coat yet? It must be uncomfortable."

Ishaan replied, "Meera is wearing my jacket. And, I am fine."

His friend replied, "Give some other sweatshirt to Meera *yaar*. Wait! Kiya's jacket is there – *wo de de.*"

Ishaan replied, "No. She's wearing the jacket she is most comfortable in. No need to ask her to change."

Saying so, Ishaan walked outside the room, taking his bag along with him.

He looked at the serenity around him. The gardens, which had sparkled with sound and glitter last night, now slept peacefully. Ishaan was just looking at the rising sun and was seeing Meera in that rising sun – yes, she was the rising business woman in the blogging industry and even when he felt that she had forgotten this fact, he remembered.

'*She is extremely hardworking; just that she gets distracted a bit easily. And if I am that distraction, I cannot be. Less people choose what they really want in life; and for me, that's the reason I respect them.*'

Just when he was thinking so, Meera came and stood near him. She said, with a smile, "Enjoying the sunrise?"

As he was about to reply, one of their friends commented, "I feel we are just five people here; because you two have hardly spoken in the whole trip. The statue in front of you is also more expressive than the two of you."

No one spoke for a minute and there was an awkward silence between them. Ishaan looked into Meera's eyes and fought the temptation to give her a hug and tell her that nothing was wrong with the silence she was keeping herself limited to. Nothing was wrong with the way she behaved and nothing was wrong in being socially awkward.

Instead, he commented rudely, "I am done with everyone. Tell her to be normal and not me."

As he left, Meera stood there alone, with tears in her eyes, expectations in her heart getting crushed miserably and her heart getting shattered into pieces. Once again.

♦

After struggling to keep her black suitcase in the cab, Meera came and occupied the back seat. All of a sudden, the warmth between the two of them was waved away with the cold vibes, all of a sudden, togetherness seemed a utopian world and all of a sudden, there was immense awkward silence between the two of them.

They were the same two people who were knitted by care a day before. But, only silence was the bond that tied them today.

As Meera looked outside the window, she thought, *'Earlier when I spoke, he felt I spoke so much. I changed that. Now, I didn't even speak a word. He still has a problem. And, what was my fault? If I am not happy, why should I pretend to be a cheerful, bubbly girl? Life doesn't work on pretence.*

As they proceeded towards the airport, there was pin drop silence in the cab; no one said a single word. Have you ever noticed how ice melts? Each conversation they had on this trip was like melting ice and then, all of a sudden, the iceberg was built, all over again. There was sunshine but once again, heavy ice fell and once again, silence heaped around the ice and once again, life was as cold as it could be to the two of them.

Sometimes, heartbreak has the power to pull you as down as it can. It was doing that for Meera. She was miserably falling in love once again, she was miserably trying hard not to fall in love and was miserably failing each time she tried. But, the only good thing about unrequited love is that it teaches perseverance. Especially for Meera, somewhere deep down in her heart, she knew she was head over heels in love with Ishaan and she also knew she could never move on because that is how she was. Whether he loved her back or not was no longer a question for her.

Ishaan looked outside the window, eyes red, filled with anger and frustration; Meera looked on the other side, her eyes too filled with anger and frustration. It was as if Ishaan was blaming himself for caring for her, and she was blaming herself for expressing what she felt. Maybe, the two of them were right in blaming themselves – because none of them had the capacity to accept the situation the way it was. Both of them wanted to tweak it as per their convenience – while she wanted that things fall in place, he wanted to destroy whatever little they had. None of them could honestly accept what the present served them. Sometimes, one should just let time decide what was best for them.

As they entered the airport and checked in, Ishaan simply walked ahead, checked in for himself and moved towards the waiting lounge, leaving Meera behind.

On the other hand, Meera did not care what anyone felt about her. She had been awake the whole night and was tired. She simply asked for the airline staff's help and checked in. Even she didn't wait for anyone and took her boarding pass.

Both of them had gone through enough emotional ups and downs in the last three days and now that things were falling apart, Meera just couldn't take it anymore.

While she had seen the best and worst of him, he had fought with his brain for the first time. For the first time, his heart wanted to rebel against logic and he forcefully wanted logic to win.

He had never fought more feelings than he did in these few days. Since forever, if he had any distraction, the easiest way to get away was to escape that person – the situation would automatically come in his control. Every time his feelings started making a way into his heart, he simply killed them. He never felt that they could reincarnate in his heart. Unlike this time, when they did – over and over.

It wasn't difficult for him to walk away. He knew he would get used to life without a person. But, this time, he just wasn't able to cut the connection between the two of them.

'*I just need to stop thinking about her,*' he told himself as he sat in front of her while waiting for the flight. Once again, both of them were glued to their phones.

This time, even Meera was annoyed. She had tried her best to make him believe that she was there for him; she did everything to not create distance but ended up being distanced from him. And to find solace, she opened her Facebook page – the perfect escape.

She had beautifully portrayed this trip to be so much fun to her followers that she ironically laughed at the fact that at least her followers thought she was having fun. She posted different pictures with her jewellery, her dupattas, her look – and had ran a story of 'The Wedding Outfit' on her page, mentioning the details of fashion and style in a winter wedding.

And, because we love weddings and the glitter, the story was a big hit on her social media. Now, she just wanted to close the campaign, and therefore, she started scrolling the screen of her phone, looking for an apt conclusion to this story.

And she found one lovely picture of hers with Ishaan. He was dressed in a black suit and she wore her blue lehenga. It was an amazing candid, and therefore, she chose it. While she was writing a beautiful caption for it, for a moment, she paused.

'*Should I ask him before posting this? He may react otherwise,*' she thought.

Therefore, attaching the image, she sent him a message on WhatsApp.

> I was thinking of closing my blog's story with this image. Cool hai na?

In a minute, the message had a blue tick. And in the next minute, his reply pinged her phone.

> Do whatever you feel like doing. Don't ask me anything... like anything ok.

In one second, that message threw her into reality. She was happily trying to distract herself in her passion, when his rudeness brought her back into the world where she wasn't cared for.

Never had he spoken to her like this earlier. What had happened now, she wondered.

She typed,

> Ok.

> But, what did I do today?

> I asked because it had you in the picture as well.

> I really tried to not make any mistake this time, but still ended up with an angry you! Just like every time. I don't know the reason. Why, Ishaan?

You know what! I never said you did something this time... it's me who is at fault. So, bye and let me be in peace now.

Meera saw the message, and simply kept the phone aside. She rested back on the couch, and could feel her eyelids wet. She wiped a drop of tear and she tried escaping reality by jumping into the memories of happinesss – where it all started – where her world had had just two names for her – Meera and Ishaan.

THE BEGINNING

Let's Break the Ice

The air was chilled, the atmosphere was ecstatic, the ice on the floor gave thrills to the adventure-lovers and the aura of the place was extremely energetic. There was ice all around and there were so many happy faces enjoying themselves.

How about you guessing which place am I talking about? 'Shimla?' you wonder?

Nope.

'Manali, maybe?' you ask.

Nope.

'Leh, then?'

Nope.

It was an ice-skating park in one of Gurgaon's largest malls, and Meera was trying to maintain her balance. Dressed in a casual pair of denim shorts and a loosely fitted t-shirt, Meera's feet struggled to hold the heavy skates that she had received before entering the skating rink. Not once had she ever tried anything as adventurous.

And when we talk about adventure, her definition was slightly different – for her, having new work at office was adventure, her blog's ups and downs were adventure, analysing the trends of her fashion journey was adventure, and spending time with herself was actual adventure. She had never even entered any ice skating rink. Forget ice skating! She had never even entered a skating rink in her life until today, when her friends had forced her to come.

'*Idiots, they got me here saying it would be fun. How is getting ten bones broken defined as fun?*' She cribbed as she struggled to walk on ice. Trust me, it was hilarious to see Meera take baby steps so cutely.

'*Had it not been Jai's birthday, I would have never even agreed to this stupid plan of his,*' she ranted.

Jai was a college friend. Meera was extremely selective with the kind of people she stayed with – choosy wouldn't be an exaggeration to define her, for that matter. The number of friends she had could be counted on fingers, but the ones she had – ask for anything and she would present it for them. Just that she was too carefree to be caught into the bonds of love, relationships and commitments. She liked being in the moment, if not rushing ahead.

Her life was as chilled as the ice was and as risk-loving as the skaters were. However, she hardly knew how to balance her body on the chilled surface. The moment she kept her foot on the ice, her balance tweaked. And just when she was about to fall, she held the railing, got up and tried again. All her friends were right in the middle of the rink, but Meera stayed aloof – that too was a typical trait. She liked doing things her way.

"Meera, come on! It isn't that hard," Jai shouted.

"Yes, sure. I don't want to get my teeth broken in the ice and if I get a fracture in my hand, who will manage my blog? I don't want to retire before I have my own fashion house."

Her friends just laughed out loud, trying to balance themselves. She was the brightness of that gang – her smile was contagious for them all. If she wasn't around, the gang would not plan out any trip. That was her place in their lives.

As Meera struggled hard to maintain her balance, her mind suggested, 'Try it out! *Tu kar legi.*'

Meera replied to her sub-conscious, '*Shut up, both of us would fall together.*'

Having said so, she took her first step away from the railing and without much ado, she fell down.

Almost all the trainers in the rink were already tired of helping her out and therefore, they just simply skated towards her with the expression of '*Not again!*'

But, they had someone else doing their job. Before they could reach, Meera had a hand to hold and get up. As he gave her his hand to hold, she looked up to him dramatically and exclaimed, "Ishaan?"

She ignored the fact that she was sitting on ice, but remembered the fact that she had to have an introduction with someone she had seen in office. She vaguely remembered the name, but she had to confirm. Getting up from the cold ice could wait, after all. ;)

Ishaan, being as simple and subtle as he was, simply smiled. By then, the skaters too had reached near her and one of them said, "Ma'am, this isn't some rocket science. It's easy. Even kids are comfortable."

"Kids have a board to hold, they know they won't fall," she retorted, still holding Ishaan's hand.

He smiled at her innocence and told the skaters, "I'll take care of her."

With the rapport which was visible between the skaters and Ishaan, it was obvious that he visited them regularly. The skater gave him a sympathetic look and left.

♦

"Ishaan, right?"

He smiled. Whenever he smiled, his eyes almost got lost in that smile. They used to shrink. And, therefore, he smiled less; apparently.

Meera continued, without any filter, "You smile as well? I've always seen you roaming with such '*gunda*'-*like* expressions in office, always!"

He smiled again. Meera was definitely enjoying this conversation over ice skating, but Ishaan loved ice skating more than words. He didn't say anything, rather asked her, offering his hand, "Come, I'll teach you skating."

"Of course not! I will fall," she replied, going back to the railing.

"Would you not try because of the fear of falling down?" he asked calmly.

And that was enough for Meera to feel challenged. She smiled and held his hand, leaving the railing behind. They walked slowly towards the centre, Ishaan directing her, "Bend both your knees, form a V-shape, and then take small steps."

While he was seriously focussed, in response Meera asked, "That is all fine. But, how do you know all this?"

He smiled at her curiosity and replied, holding her carefully, "I like skating."

Meera smiled broadly at him. "Nice."

He said, "Carefully leave my hand now."

"Why? I'll fall if I leave you," she retorted.

Looking at her cheerfulness, for a second, Ishaan forgot he had to skate. He smiled and happily held her hand for the next thirty minutes. He probably didn't realise, but it was the first time he had parted with his time of skating for someone he knew nothing about – or probably just the name and the fact that they were in the same office.

Strangely, it was the first time he loved being in the company that was exactly opposite to his. If he spoke a single word in ten minutes, she could speak ten sentences in one minute. Meera asked every single question which came to her mind, without any filter.

"So, you are a software developer in Apticon, right?"

Apticon Solutions was the company that hired Meera six months back from campus. And it was the same company that hired Ishaan from his campus four years back. At twenty-two and twenty-six, they were two of the most valued employees – any company would like dedicated workers, after all.

"Yes," he replied.

"You must have done engineering, then?" she asked chirpily.

"Yes," he replied.

"That's nice," she said.

"Nothing is that nice about it." He smiled.

"Why?"

"You ask too many questions. Concentrate on ice skating for now!"

She smiled and was about to say something else, when her right feet lost balance and the two of them were on the ice floor, once again. The only difference was that this time Meera's head was on his chest and they were so close that she could hear his heartbeats. For a moment, their eyes were locked in each other's and Meera could trace all his features carefully.

In between the ice skating rink, amidst people who were struggling with skates, in between the trainers and in between the awkwardness, Meera was lost in his eyes – until he made a remark, to break the silence between them.

"Never have I fallen here since the last two years. *Bezzati karwa di.*"

Meera laughed and asked him to pick her up. Falling, tripling, falling again and finally reaching the corner, their first conversation came to an end.

As they came and sat outside the rink, Meera and Ishaan removed their skates, and it was then that Ishaan asked the first question of the evening.

"You might not have come alone?"

"Of course not! It's my friend's birthday and he loves stupid adventures, and because it was his birthday, I had to listen to him and come. And you know what? In between all of this, these guys just went upstairs to get pictures clicked."

'*Whoa! She can speak non-stop, for hours. I always thought she was a quiet one.*' Ishaan smiled at her art of answering in two hundred words when twenty could do.

'*She must have been the student who wrote ten pages for answering a two-mark question.*' He commented in his mind and smiled again. More than he spoke to others, he spoke to himself in his thoughts.

"Good. Then, I will take your leave. See you in office," was all that he said.

He gave his hand forward for a shake, while Meera had both her arms open to give him a parting hug. Meera laughed to break the awkwardness and shook hands with him before he left.

Somewhere deep down in the two minds was a question, "The evening was good. Wasn't it?"

Office Office

Giving a little context to Meera and Ishaan's life, here was the only connect between them – Apticon Solutions, which was a blogging company, standing in the industry for the last ten years. It was one of those companies that had used the platform for digital when nothing else was digital. As a result of which, it stood as one of India's leading content companies. They created marketing content for different clients.

Meera was hired as an intern for a year from her campus selections, while Ishaan was recruited as a developer four years back. Knowing Meera well, you would know how much she enjoyed new situations every day and that was the kick that kept her engaged in her office. It had been six months that Meera had joined office and keeping in mind her flamboyant personality, quite a lot of people noticed her entry at the workplace. She would have conversations with a lot of people about her blog, her writing, her passion.

While Ishaan stayed in his own comfort zone, Meera was someone who would talk to almost everyone she could. Except of course when she was zoned out, which was quite often. Strangely, even when Ishaan knew her, visited a few colleagues near her workstation and spoke to them, he never thought of brewing a conversation with her. It was perhaps too much for him to do – until the previous evening, when they met in the ice skating rink!

◆

'Meera Tiwari' he typed on the search bar of his Skype chat.

I am sure those who work in corporate would know how important this chat device is. It can cure escalation emails too. My manager used to say, 'interpersonal communication always helps!'

While he selected her name on the window and typed, "Hey, good morning," Meera was just told that her internship was extended for a year based on her performance, and the news made her elated.

"Happy happy morning, Mr Skater."

It was 20th December, a chilly morning in the National Capital of India and the morning had resulted to be a great one for Meera.

Ishaan smiled, imagining her cheerful tone behind the message. He wrote, taking a look at his watch. "I have a little headache. Want to go to get some tea?"

It was 11 a.m., exactly when Meera went upstairs to the cafeteria to have her cup of coffee. Hence, she replied immediately, "Hey, sure. I just have to meet someone and then will see you at your workstation. We can go upstairs then. Sounds okay?"

"Ok."

'*Who replies with just an ok?*' she thought, but then she had too much to focus on except for this 'ok'.

They were poles apart; one was such a miser of words that he saved as many as he could, even when he was typing, and the other wrote odes while messaging.

Anyway, just when Meera was about to get up, a few colleagues of her came and as she started talking, she forgot she had to meet someone in the next five minutes. He was, after all, just a new colleague who she had met a day before. It was allowed to forget in this case. *Or, maybe not!*

She chirpily spoke to her friends, enjoyed her moment and then started working on the project which was nearing its completion. She had successfully delivered 189 articles in 5 months. No wonder they wanted to retain her. She worked on an article on sports and when she was about to wrap up for the day and was closing all windows, she saw Ishaan's message.

'Damn. I forgot to meet him!'

She quickly packed her bag and ran to his workstation, which was on the first floor.

In a blink of the eyes, she was at his workstation, with a brown sling bag hanging on her shoulders. When Meera reached there, Ishaan was carefully focussing on his screen. She didn't say a word but stood there for him to complete whatever he was doing. When Meera knew she was at fault, she generally became too sweet all of a sudden.

Meera was always bad with science and technology. She knew she would just ask lame questions and looking at the guilt-struck situation, she didn't want to annoy him further. She just stood there patiently till Ishaan looked up at her and smiled formally.

"Hey, I am really sorry," she whispered.

"For?" he asked, still working.

"I forgot." She smiled sheepishly.

In a simple kurta and a pair of jeans with small earrings hanging innocently from her ears, she looked pretty. Ishaan smiled and said, "That's okay. Some other day, maybe."

Void, she could feel it and that was one thing Meera was

scared of. She could handle conflicts, emotional breakdowns, problems – but she was scared of silence creating distance between people. Cancerians are in love with loyalty and relationships. They can't let go of friendships easily. And with Ishaan, There was a special bond she could feel instantly.

Meera replied, "I know you are swarmed with work...," looking at his screen with animated expressions, she said, "... and I wouldn't understand even a bit of your work. But, if you can steal ten minutes out, can we have tea together?"

"You'll get late, Meera," He said in a caring tone, still looking at his screen.

Meera replied, "That's okay. Let's go?"

He was about to say something when one of his team members too got up and said, "Ishaan sir, take a break. You haven't got up since morning. We are all going to the canteen. You want to join us?"

Ishaan turned to them and said, "You guys continue. I'll join you later."

When he had his back towards Meera, she couldn't hear even a single word. She asked, "What did you tell them?"

Ishaan laughed. If he spoke in the slightest tone possible, Meera had a loudspeaker inbuilt in her throat. He said, "Not everyone can be as loud as you are, you know."

Meera retorted, while he locked his computer, finally breaking the eye contact with his screen, "Just because you speak in whispers doesn't mean that the whole world has to speak like that, sir." She had said 'Sir' deliberately.

"Hence, just because you compete with a loudspeaker, doesn't mean that the world too has to join that competition," he replied with a smile as they climbed the stairs to reach their office's cafeteria.

◆

The architect for this office was definitely a man of creativity. And, while his creativity wasn't evidently visible in the workstations, it was definitely overflowing at the cafeteria. As Ishaan and Meera stood in front of the cafeteria, the ambience was lovely. Fewer offices have a roof-top cafeteria, after all. The dim lights created a subtle effect during winters, the wooden furnishing added to the ambience, which was serene and calm. This was the place that saw all the ups and downs in an employee's life, after all.

As Meera and Ishaan walked ahead and took a table in a comparatively vacant corner, Ishaan asked, "What would you have with tea?"

"Anything," she replied.

"How do I decide?" he asked, inquisitive of the fact that the girl trusted his choice of food so much even when they had come out for the first time.

"I don't like looking at menus. You can choose anything," she said confidently.

He sat down in front of her and started reading the options that they had. "White sauce pasta?" he asked, considering it was his favourite.

"Who eats white sauce pasta in office?" she replied. Ishaan felt a little offended for his favourite dish, but because he never said anything, he didn't say anything this time too.

"Sandwich, maybe?" he tried a safer option, but was eliminated again.

"No," she said outright.

"My head?" he asked, with a smirk.

That was the first time she saw him joking a bit, therefore, she said, "I might consider this option, though." She added politely, "I am sorry. Let's have French fries."

Ishaan was about to get up, when Meera got up, took her wallet and started moving towards the counters. She said, while she walked, "You sit, you already look tired. I'll go and get our food."

Yes, he was tired. And therefore, he didn't pretend to be gallant and well-equipped with manners. He sat there while she brought two plates of French fries with two *masala chai*.

She smiled as she kept the plate in front of him and he thanked her with his million dollar smile. "Thank you, Miss Blogger," he said.

Meera smiled as she dipped her French fries in the ocean of sauce that she had created. As Ishaan looked at her, he admired the hardwork that she did to balance her job with her passion for fashion blogging. He wasn't among those who would express what he felt at one go. He would take time, analyse if what he felt was right or not and then would 'think' about expressing it.

He was someone who would happily hear what the person in front of him had to say, endlessly. He was an extremely good listener. And Meera – she was an extremely good speaker. She had odes and tales to speak when she was comfortable with someone, and strangely, with him, she felt that connect right from the beginning, which generally wasn't the case with her.

"Today, I had a meeting in the morning. These guys have extended my tenure for a year. But, they were planning a project change for me. I am slightly nervous and much more than that, I am upset, because I'll have to leave a team behind." She narrated the whole day's events to him, who heard her with complete interest. Her innocence was something he was immediately impressed by, and amused as well.

He replied, "You aren't moving to some other world. Relax!"

She smiled sheepishly and added, "I am scared of changing a zone. It took me six months to be familiar with this place and…"

"...and as you got familiar here, you will get used to that team as well. Just let yourself a little free of over-thinking and apprehensions," he intervened.

Meera smiled, replying, "True! I think *I think too much*. You tell, what's going on in your project?"

"Everything is as usual," was all that he had to say.

If she was a story, he was the expressions which never expressed themselves. If she was the word, he was the silence between the words. They were poles apart and the fun fact was that after today's conversation, both of them realised this fact clearly. Meera was a chatterbox when she wanted to be, she was socially awkward when she wasn't a chatterbox, she zoned out frequently and was someone who feared void and change. Ishaan was calm, so much so that nothing could worry him – or probably that is what he liked telling people. His peaceful nature calmed his mind and his mind was where all the talking took place, because he never spoke what was discussed in the confidential meeting of his mind. In fact, he did not even share the minutes of the meeting with anyone.

In the dim light and breezy cold winds, there was a little friendship brewing. Or perhaps, just some colleague-connect. Meera didn't care; she was the same with almost everyone she liked, and hence, she simply got up and left office happily, seeing him off at his workstation and walked to her nest like the free bird that she was.

Ishaan, on the other hand, got back to work. For him, he never lost focus. If he was working, the world could be on fire and he wouldn't care.

Two ways, two people and two different lifestyles – they moved on into their different roads, happily and casually!

Metro se chalien?

> Hope you reached?

He typed on Facebook messenger while he sat in the office cab at 9: 30 p.m.

He did not have her phone number and being himself, he wanted to ensure that she had reached safely. He thought for a millisecond and then sent the message.

Meera looked at the message while she was unlocking her flat in Mayur Vihar, where she stayed with Kavya, her little sister. She replied, while juggling with the keys, the locks and the handle of the door.

> Yup!

> Where do you stay?

'*Remembered a little too soon?*' she smirked and replied,

> Mayur Vihar Phase 1. It is near Akshardham.

I know where Mayur Vihar is, Meera.

Meera read his message and for a second, she sheepishly told herself, '*He isn't an outsider to the city like you are; he lives here since he was in class 5th.*'

What about you? Left office or still flirting with your desktop?

He, now much into the conversation did not even lock his phone after sending the last message. He knew, she would reply instantly.

After reading her message, he smiled. '*This girl has an aura of positivity around her. I don't know what it is, but there is something that is special about Meera. Maybe her zeal, maybe—*'

Just when he was thinking about her, she messaged again.

There?

You realise people take time in typing, don't you?

And yes, I am now free to flirt with anyone else, since I have left my desktop and moved on. 😂.

Meera, who by now was inside her room, under her blanket, smiled at his reply.

So, you reached home?"

Nope, 20 minutes more.

Whoa! Where do you stay? London?

> Heard of Inderlok?

> I think it's near London, but where exactly?

'*You can't even name five proper places in Delhi and here you are asking him his exact location,*' her mind scolded her, and like always, she ignored it.

While she was chatting to Ishaan, Kavya came in the room and settling on the bed, she calculated her sister's expressions and in exactly ten seconds, she asked, "There's something new brewing here?"

"Of course not! Just a colleague I was chatting with," Meera replied.

"I haven't seen you so intrigued while talking to other colleagues?" Kavya questioned.

Meera gave her a disgusted look and replied, "You have the potential to replace ACP Pradyuman from *CID*, bro. This is just a random friend in office and you know how I am, I just don't care much about people."

"Unfortunately, yes! That's the reason you are single since forever," Kavya replied.

"Happily, though," Meera added and then got back to her conversation with Ishaan.

> East Delhi. I think you can do with this information.

He replied analysing the fact that Meera knew nothing about the city she did her graduation from.

> Yes, I know little about roads.
> But, I am an expert of Delhi
> Metro. Ask me anything and I
> would know.

He then thought about how dedicated she would have been that even when she had the freedom of doing whatever she liked, she still didn't waste any time. He had silently started to like the madness Meera had for her profession.

> Chalo, that's fine. And, I'll see
> you. I have to look at some
> little things in my new blog.

It was already 11 p.m. and she was about to begin her work. Ishaan bid her a good night and kept his phone aside. He was about to fall asleep when he thought, '*I tend to return from office and just sleep – and I always thought everyone who came to office did exactly the same – either they partied or they went home and saw some good series and slept. What is this girl made of? She is too hardworking and is perfect – she manages work efficiently in office and then works so minutely on her writing at home! I respect her hardwork.*'

Thinking about her positivity and zeal to achieve her dreams, he slept!

'I am an expert of the Metro, Ishaan.'

It was 7:10 a.m. and the Tiwari house looked quiet, with the two sisters happily dreaming in their sleep. The two of them generally left for work and school together at 6:45. Meera took her office cab and Kavya took her school bus. Unfortunately, both of them missed their buses today.

When, at 7:15, Meera opened her eyes and looked out of the blanket, she panicked, "Kavu, get up. It is 7:15 already."

Kavya was in no mood to even open her eyes and trust me, it wasn't even her fault – she was in Delhi, the chilled capital of India. It was 7 degrees outside and lazing around in the comfortable round bed was the option anyone would first choose. She replied, "Didi, I am not going to school today. Let me sleep in peace."

"Of course not, ask Mumma first."

Well, their parents, Smriti and Manav owned a car showroom in Mumbai and stayed there. Meera, when she cleared her class 12th, wanted to pursue her education from Delhi University and hence, she shifted to Delhi. Kavya, being her shadow, wanted to move in with her sister, and therefore, they came to stay together in one of their flats, which had been vacant till now.

The distance might be in thousands, but the bond these girls shared with their parents was unimaginable. No matter what happened, their parents were their go-to person. Kavya, being the younger one, always got the benefit of the Universal Younger rule, even with Meera.

She said, "All of this wouldn't have happened if you did not have all the late night chats with alleged new colleagues. I missed my bus because of you. Only if you had been responsible…"

Throwing her towel at her, Meera smiled, and then retorted, "You are such a drama queen."

"Yes, that I am," Kavya said, smirked and sneaked her head under the blanket again.

◆

Meera quickly wore a casual t-shirt and jeans, put on her colourful socks and quickly wore her blue hoodie. She was getting ready at an unbelievable speed. And as she applied some essentials, she saw a message on Facebook messenger. Keeping the time in mind, she quickly ignored it and rushed to leave home. As she locked the door, there was another notification and she quickly glanced at it.

"Hey, good morning." The message said. And, yes, it was the hero of this story.

Meera didn't send a reply, but called him on Facebook, "Ishaan, I missed my bus today. I just started right now. It is also my first day in the new project and I will reach late. I am such an idiot, a sloth. I—"

He was happy to hear her cheerful voice right in the morning, but he was more amused to hear her non-stop banter. He replied, "Shh! Relax. I am in the Metro. See me at Udyod Bhawan. I'll get down and wait for you."

He knew she needed to be calmed down before she reached her new project manager, and when it came to calmness, Ishaan knew he was a pro.

Meera repied, huffing and puffing, looking for an auto, "You will also get late because of me…"

Again, she was cut short, when he said, "I'll wait."

Keeping the phone, he thought, *'She's just one amusing human being. But, however she is, she is a balloon of positivity.'*

As he thought about her, she rushed and reached Rajiv Chowk, the hub of all the metro lines.

◆

Travelling in the Metro after six long months, Meera was extremely nostalgic of the times when she was super carefree and wrote all her fashion stories and blogs while travelling alone. She never liked company while she travelled. She loved being alone, and enjoyed her solitude.

While in a hurry, she quickly took the metro towards her college, which was in the opposite direction to where Ishaan stood waiting. Just when the door of the Metro closed, Ishaan called. Poor chap, he had been waiting for her for thirty-five minutes now.

"*Kaha pahuche aap?*" he asked.

"Next station is New Delhi," she replied confidently and in the next millisecond, when the two of them exclaimed together is when she realised that she had taken the wrong metro.

"Damn, I am sorry Ishaan. I forgot I wasn't going to the college. I am such a…"

She was about to get into her self-critique mode, when Ishaan laughed and directed her, "Get down and meet me at Udyog Bhavan. Take the next metro from the opposite side..."

"I know how to come towards Udyog Bhavan, Ishaan," she replied and cursed herself twenty more times.

Meera shook her head, crowning herself as the biggest idiot in the universe. When she travelled alone, she was pretty sure of ways, but today, when it was the first time she was travelling with him, she had not failed to create an image that assured him that she was world's biggest big mouth, but knew nothing.

'What would he think of me? I am such an idiot!' she mumbled in her head as she took the metro towards him.

He, on the other hand, was literally amused by her personality. As he patiently waited for her, he thought, *'I know she is imperfect, I know she is a misfit, but she is one person I don't feel like judging. She is at least carrying her true self on her, unlike the world, which just pretends. I think her innocence is her biggest USP.'*

He smiled as he saw so many people run in their daily routine. Delhi metro could be labelled as one of the most crowded places and while Ishaan travelled in it since the last three years, he never got a chance to stop and observe. The new girl in his life was giving him a perspective, maybe.

'Everyone rushes every day, but only few have the guts to chase their dreams. I am so proud of Meera that she manages everything so perfectly. In her age, it's commendable.'

Just when he was praising her in his mind, she came rushing towards him and stood next to him, huffing and puffing. He just could not hide his feelings and burst out laughing.

♦

The chain of Meera's jacket was open, her hair looked amazingly messy and her forehead had drops of sweat dancing. She looked funny. So much so that if she just went and stood on a comedy stage, people would have laughed.

"What?" she asked sheepishly.

Ishaan laughed and asked, "And someone knew everything about the Delhi metro."

Meera looked embarrassed and guilty of making him wait and looking at her puppy face, he said, with a smile, "It is okay. We are allowed to make mistakes. Don't feel embarrassed."

For once, he himself wasn't sure if he was saying this. He was someone who aimed for perfection and embraced it. For once, even he doubted why he was being good to this imperfect fellow. But, he just enjoyed her company and said, "I haven't laughed this hard in the last few months. You compensated for the delay."

Meera smiled brightly at him on hearing this and as they boarded the metro, the little kid in her was back.

◆

Generally, in winters, when you have all your jackets and coats over you, the temperature inside the metro is a little uncomfortable. You tend to get irritated by the variation in the temperature, and so did Meera. She wanted to remove her socks.

Quite an important task to do when you are travelling with a new colleague for the first time, right? But Meera, being Meera, couldn't stand herself being uncomfortable. She bent and took off her magenta pink and dark blue socks and was then thinking of where to keep them, when she thought he didn't notice but, well – he noticed everything.

Ishaan smiled and registered how cutely she was trying to hide her socks, and noticing her discomfort with him around, he said, "I wouldn't mind keeping a kid's socks in my bag. Give them to me. And I am hoping they are clean."

Meera was startled knowing that he observed her. She replied, "Of course they are clean. But, I am just a little apprehensive of whether I can keep this with my laptop. It is my writing, right?"

Ishaan was impressed. He took the socks and kept it in the side pocket of his bag, saying, "Few people respect their passion and I really respect them."

For the first time, Meera was smiling genuinely, without any apprehension of being judged or without any fear of not being accepted as a friend. She was happily happy to see him appreciating her, and while she received a lot of appreciations from her followers on social media and colleagues in office, she saw genuine words in someone's praise for the first time. She definitely could not hide the happiness that the moment brought for her. In a moment, Ishaan became someone who mattered to her.

That is how Meera was – she would get attached easily and then would never let go of that attachment.

'Let's go out, Ishaan?'

It was Meera's first day into the new project, and without any induction, she was asked to deliver an article for a completely new client. Throughout the eight hours of work, adding three more hours of late stay, she completed the article with media and animations. She designed the whole article with the colour scheme she used for the previous client and she knew it always worked.

However, when she was about to send it for her supervisor's review, her boss asked, "What is this?"

"My article," Meera replied.

"And why is this so colourful? Did you not know that our client is super finicky about using bright colours?" Her supervisor snapped.

"I wasn't informed about this requirement," Meera mumbled, feeling humiliated by the way she was given her feedback.

"It isn't school anymore, right? I have twenty other things on my plate. It was your work, you could have asked for the branding," was the clear cut reply.

Meera was extremely intimidated by the way her supervisor spoke to her. But, just because she didn't want to spoil her rapport on the very first day, she did not argue. She silently kept her anger inside her as she replied, "I am sorry. I'll update this. Please provide me with the client requirement document."

"You don't even know where that is and you started working. Wow!" Her supervisor sarcastically said while packing her bag and leaving office.

"Do it tomorrow now!" she added as she started to leave.

While for Sadhna, it was just a new intern she was shouting at and making her better, for Meera, this was insult – sure shot insult. And for someone whose work was her strength, this was heartbreaking.

'*What the fuck does she think of herself? She's a bitch.*' Meera spoke to herself as she was closing the tabs of the windows open in her system.

She wasn't among those who would learn and remember things when they were told in a strict manner. Rather, she got disappointed, dejected and heartbroken when it was about her work.

Just before she was switching her system off, she checked if Ishaan was online and when she found the green sign in front of his name on her screen, she felt reassured. Her heart wanted peace and she was glad she knew the most peaceful person around.

Even when it was 8:45 p.m., Meera did not want to stay alone and travel for two hours. She just wanted to go to someone who could make her feel better, and for some strange reason, he was right there. Her instincts just instructed her to do what she did next.

She picked up her sling bag, pulled her coat from the seat and walked towards the first floor. She walked speedily towards his workstation. He was yet again staring at his screen with concentration and she was yet again standing next to him. The only difference was that her eyes had tons to speak.

The moment Ishaan looked at her, he registered that her eyes were extremely expressive. He started, "Hey Miss Blogger. *Kya haal chaal?*"

Meera did not say a single word, but kept staring at his desk. For her, it was a situation that had never happened before – she was never questioned about work the way she was questioned today and having never faced any failure, she did not know how to handle this.

For him too, it was a situation that had never happened before – never did anyone walk up to him as a confidant. And, he did not know how to make her smile; he was bad with his knowledge about girls, after all!

He got up and then standing in front of her, he asked, "Meera, is everything okay?"

Meera did not speak a single word; she just sobbed. She was crying over one conversation with her supervisor. And Ishaan was all the more uncomfortable seeing her like this. He had always seen her as someone who was confident and enthusiastic. Plus, they were in office.

However, he was still calm. "Give me a second. Let's go to the cafeteria and talk."

And as soon as he turned toward the cafeteria, Meera held his wrist and said, "I don't want to stay in this stupid place even for a second."

Ishaan looked at his watch. He had booked a cab for 9 p.m. and it was already 8:50. He knew if he missed this cab, he would reach home by midnight by the metro and his rational thinking just did not allow him to do that. His mind kept telling him that he should console her for a minute and then, as he always did, he should leave.

'*It'll be late. Leave, Ishaan.*' His mind directed him.

"Sure. Come, let's go out. We'll then see where to go," he said instead.

So, someone who never bothered to care, actually cared. For the first time, he wanted to hold her hand and take her out of the mess that she was in.

♦

As they stepped out of office, Ishaan booked a cab for the two of them and asked her, "You are fond of sweets, aren't you?"

Meera nodded with puffy eyes. "But, I don't want to eat anything," she said, placing a sad look on her face.

"That I'll manage. You just tell me one thing, how will you go home after 10?" he asked.

"By Metro," she replied, wryly.

Just then, Ishaan messaged his brother,

> I'll be very late. I have to drop someone at Mayur Vihar first.

It's interesting how he took that decision in a millisecond. It is even more interesting how his mind behaved in an exactly opposite manner to what it always did.

As they sat in the cab, he asked, "*Achha,* so you won't say anything, right?"

Turning to the cab driver, he said, "*Bhaiya radio hi laga do. Madam toh baat karengi nahi.*"

As the driver switched on the radio, he played the saddest songs that he could, listening to which, Ishaan whispered, "Your story would at least be a little more engaging than these songs, I am assuming."

Meera smiled, for the first time in the whole evening. Then, she narrated the whole story to him – about Sadhna, her attitude and the unpleasant day.

"...I really don't understand how she could just blame me for a mistake I never did. It is unfair," she completed her story.

"Meera, I thought you were intelligent. You are affected by this tiny, little thing?" he asked, surprised.

"Tiny? You find this as a tiny problem?" she questioned.

"Of course not! I just don't see any problem in this tiny situation," he answered.

'*What the hell is wrong with this person?*' she thought. '*How could he not see a problem in this extremely problematic situation?*' Her mind continued to pop questions.

♦

And while she was communicating with her mind, they reached Dunkin' Donuts at Huda City Centre. Ishaan said as they ordered eight donuts, "You'll love these donuts."

"I don't know if I will, but I can clearly see your love for them," she replied with a little smile popping from her lips.

He smiled broadly and replied, "I love sweets. You know what, Blogger? I feel that food solves everything. And hence, whenever in problem, just turn to food."

Meera laughed. She then asked, "You said there is no problem that you could find in my situation. How do you get to decide that for my life? *Itne bhi genius nahi ho aap.*"

Ishaan carefully looked at her and replied, "Who are you?"

"Meera. But, what kind of stupid, Bollywoodish-philosophical question is that? You think you'll ask me who I am; then you'll say '*Tu beer hai*', then, like TVF Pitchers, you will explain that *mein beer kyun hun*," she blabbered.

"Or are you Kabir Khan from *Chak De* – oh, wait; you look like him at times," she added.

By the way, she was serious when she said she saw the Kabir Khan look from *Chak De India* in him. Ishaan ignored her and asked again, "Shut up. Answer the next question. When you listen to your name, 'Meera Tiwari', what is the first image that comes to your mind?"

"My blog," she replied in the quickest time.

He smiled listening to this answer. Had she said anything else, he would have been disappointed. "Good. Now tell me one thing. Whatever this supervisor of yours said, does it anywhere hamper your blog?" He asked, eating his third donut. Mind you, his words would stop, but not his donuts.

"Nope," she replied, after thinking for a second.

"Then how do you even see this as a problem?" he asked.

Meera smiled broadly as she said, "Exactly. It shouldn't matter, right?"

"Of course not, you idiot," he replied with a broad smile that once again shrunk his eyes. He said, "See, you have to realise that you are much above this office. You know that you have achieved quite a bit at this age. There are many people for whom the ultimate ambition is to be where you already are – you are a social media influencer, a fashion blogger, who is followed by so many youngsters. People desperately crave for such attention, Meera. Start seeing that as a priority and everything else would automatically become insignificant."

As he said so, Meera replied, "My work is my priority, for sure. But, how can one stay in an environment with such negativity?"

"I'll try and beat the negativity for you, I promise. You just focus on achieving your dreams. Not everyone has the guts to see such big dreams, after all."

As he said so, there was a charm in his eyes and an assurance in hers. For once, everything that happened at work with her supervisor did not matter and for the first time, Meera was sure of the next day. Not because of herself, but because of him. She knew she had someone she could fall back on, if not on herself.

Sometimes, if you want to hold a hand to help you walk ahead, I don't think it's being dependent. Yes, ultimately, it is *you* who comes out of every situation and if someone helps you pass through, that's not being less of independent. A lot of times, we just tend to believe that if you dream high, you can't rely on anyone; but sometimes, I think situations make it inevitable. **#Gyan**

♦

It was already 10:15 p.m. by the time Ishaan gulped in seven donuts and Meera managed to finish just one; that too with his help. He said, looking at his brown strapped watch, "Let's go. It's already late."

Meera nodded and with a smile, they left Huda City Centre, the metro station nearest to their office. When Meera had put her first step in the place, it was with tears, tension and taunts revolving in her mind. And now that she boarded the metro, it was with charm, cheer and calm.

As they walked into a comparatively empty metro, Ishaan said, "We still have an hour-and-a-half to reach your metro station, why don't you write till then?"

"In the metro? How do I write here?" she questioned.

Ishaan gave her a look – the epic Ishaan look, and then took out her laptop from her bag, saying, "How do you write at home? Take out the laptop, keep it on your lap and start writing."

"But you—"

She was about to complete her thought, when he intervened, "I am very sleepy. I'll sleep."

Meera gave him her typical complaining look. "How can you sleep when you have a co-traveller?"

Ishaan smirked and switching the laptop for her, saying, "Because my co-traveller will travel with her dreams now."

Writing, or anything creative, isn't just a task that you have to accomplish. I agree, it cannot be done till the heart shouts out loudly to tell you to 'WRITE'. But, sometimes, it's not about the heart – it's about the situation around you. Today, it wasn't that Meera was a little less ambitious about her passion. It was just that she was a little distracted by situations around her.

What she would be vulnerable to was frustration. Ishaan saw it in her eyes today and he simply wanted to keep her away from those distractions. He did not doubt her abilities to achieve her dreams, but was sceptical of the corporate environment she was in. It was always difficult to turn a dream into reality, he knew.

Today, he just wanted to push her to write, because he knew that it was the only way she would feel a little less troubled. Otherwise, he knew there would have been flood all around.

Strangely, some people, sometimes become your companion on the path of your dreams. You don't owe them anything, but your dreams owe them a lot. I think it's all about those people at times when nothing works, something begins to work!

◆

As the metro stopped at Rajiv Chowk at 11 p.m., Meera got up to leave. In the next second, Ishaan got up as well.

Meera said authoritatively, "I have gone home at midnight as well. You are not coming anywhere."

She had been a free bird – someone who wouldn't care a lot about the world and roam at her pace. Whatever she wanted, she would happily go alone and explore it. She wasn't a damsel in distress who wanted a prince charming to look after her. She could manage her commutes.

On the other hand, he knew how she had lived her life. He had no doubts that Meera could go home alone. And, he was the least gallant person on earth to follow stereotypes. It was just that his heart wanted to be with her and hence, all the effort.

Even when his heart said he wanted her company more, he didn't accept that. For his external self, it was concern he had towards a colleague. Masks and masquerades, ah!

He did not bother arguing with her. He just stood quietly as she kept telling him to go and sit. When Rajiv Chowk came, Ishaan quietly got down with her and started walking, till the gates of the metro closed.

Meera impulsively made a comment, "I really don't like people policing my life. I am someone who likes being on myself."

Poor him! He stopped for a minute, turned to her and looking straight in her hazel eyes, replied, "I am not being a patriarch who wants to protect you till you reach home, but I can be a good friend, right?"

Ishaan thought he was convincing. Little did he know that convincing her was the toughest job on earth.

"Wrong. Friendship is never built on burdens, Ishaan," she replied.

'*Her theories need refinement,*' he thought as he walked with a taut face.

One, Ishaan couldn't understand why he was being the superman today, why his heart wanted to control his mind and why his mind was giving up against his heart. Two, she was being obnoxious. He wanted to leave, but his heart still wanted him to stay.

'*Had it been anyone else, I would have never let her call me a patriarch. Stop taking her tantrums and leave right away,*' his mind directed.

'*But, perhaps, Meera doesn't mean what she always says. She's innocent and says whatever comes to her mind. That is a rare habit,*' his mind defended.

And in this conversation, the defender was able to save the goal.

While they walked towards the metro, neither of them spoke anything. Meera was aggressive and stubborn. And Ishaan was a passive stubborn.

As they boarded the last metro, Ishaan said, "At times, it is okay to be a little selfless, Meera."

"I am sorry, I cannot be," she replied, angrily.

"You are. But, you are too busy pretending to the world that you are not," he declared patting on her head. He then added, "So, if I am in need of a friend, dying somewhere in the deserts, would you not come to my rescue?"

Meera gave him a disgusted look and replied, "If you are coming with me to my place, then you stay there over night. Else, walk down and take the metro to your house."

"We'll decide that later..." He tried to say, when she stopped walking and said, "We decide that right now, else I am not walking a step ahead."

Her eyes had a spark when she was angry. That spark was dangerous, he quickly registered. He also knew that she was a nasty kid when it came to getting her tantrums approved. He knew arguing with her would not help.

'She could compete with my two-year-old niece when it came to being ziddi,' He told himself.

He knew that they did not have a lot of time to waste, considering that the last metro was at 11:32 p.m., he said, "Okay, I'll stay. But, I hope my safety is not at risk. You know how good looking I am..."

Meera looked at him and with a smirk, she made an extremely funny face. "Blah blah blah," she imitated.

As they walked, Meera slightly lifted her chin and looked at him from the corner of her right eye. There was something in Ishaan that was magnetising her attention towards him, and the problem was, it wasn't just his good looks. He was the simplest of all, but something, somewhere was different in him – maybe the art of convincing her, she thought and pricked the thought bubbles that her mind was forming.

◆

Amidst the mist and chilly breezes of December, Meera and Ishaan reached her apartment at around midnight. As she was about to press the doorbell, Ishaan held her hand. Meera looked at him with suspicious eyes. To that look, he replied with a soft answer, "Your sister must have slept. Let's not disturb her."

Meera looked at him and laughed loudly, replying, "You care too much, Ishaan. My sister is an insomniac; she would be watching *Riverdale*. It's me who asks her to sleep, else she can watch her series for the whole night…"

Saying so, Meera pressed the bell once, twice and five times in one go.

Kavya, who by the way had slept while watching her favourite series, came with sleepy eyes and a disgusted expression on her face. "I wish Mom-Dad had put curfew timings for you. You've just become too *awara*, di," she said, not realising that her sister had brought a colleague home.

As she said so, Ishaan laughed at the embarrassing expressions Meera had. After he had enjoyed Meera's expressions, he looked at the other side of the door, to find a petite young girl with messy hair and a gray batman night suit. Even before he entered their apartment, he said, "Nice outfit, I must say."

That was the exact moment where the awkward 'guest-like' silence broke and Kavya laughed loudly. She said, "If you find this interesting, *didi's* dresses would amuse you multi-fold."

"They already do. I saw those magenta socks today."

And the two of them again laughed together. Ishaan then took a step ahead and putting his hand forward, he said, "I am Ishaan."

"And I am Kavya," she said, shaking his hand and smiling broadly while Meera went to change into her lower and sweatshirt.

As she walked towards Ishaan and Kavya, she looked amusing in a sweatshirt that had rabbits made on it and a light pink lower. Ishaan didn't forget to notice the magenta socks and laughed, commenting, "Her wardrobe looks like a colour palette, Kavya." He quickly added, "And the print – my niece, Anamika, too wears better prints."

It was the first time Ishaan opened up.

"That's what. You should look at mine – it is all black and gray. And this one doesn't even spare a single colour," Kavya added.

As Meera came and sat with the two of them, she said with a taut face, "People like colours. And, that is completely fine."

"Of course, when did we say it is not? We were just discussing—" Ishaan tried to speak with earnest expressions, when he was cut midway by Meera, "Okay, let's go to bed now. Kavu, *chalo* – go sleep."

"Shut up! Stop being a boring sister. We are playing Koffee with Kavya," Kavya ordered and then looked at Ishaan with a request to play along. Undoubtedly, Ishaan agreed and gave her a loud high-five. He loved the way Kavya was – innocent, sweet, simple and admirable.

The way she looked at him, seeking approval for her idea, with the assurance of getting it approved – took his heart. She was a kid, who he instantly wanted to look after.

In that little moment, he found a sister and Kavya found a partner in crime against her sister!

What a team!

There are a lot of relations which cannot and should not be knitted into forceful names. They are good the way they are. Ishaan and Kavya's was just one of those beautiful relations!

Koffee with Kavya

It was 1:15 a.m. by the clock, 8 degrees by the phone app, and 125% excitement level reflected Ishaan and Kavya's faces. Meera knew her sister could gel with anyone in a minute, but she also knew that Kavya never felt bonded with someone so quickly. For the first time, she could see her bonding with someone at this speed.

At the same time, she saw the other side of Ishaan with Kavya. She could see a kid jumping with excitement, a child bloating with joy and a friend hoping to be himself.

"Meera, come, you and I are her guests for tonight," he said, pretty excited.

Meera walked with a cup of coffee and sat beside him on their round bed. The three of them sat with folded legs with the blanket giving them warmth.

Kavya imitated Karan Johar, and started off like he does in his show *Koffee with Karan*. "So, good evening everyone. Today we have two extremely awesome guests with us. Our first guest is a remarkable Maggi maker, a super cool brother and a fresh breeze of air. And accompanying him is Meera Tiwari, someone I have been tolerating since childhood and I am bored of. But because she is Ishaan's friend, I'll tolerate her on my show. Welcome Meera and Ishaan."

As she said so, Meera threw a pillow at Kavya, making an angry frown. Ishaan winked at her.

Kavya asked a couple of interesting questions and was all set to ask the next one, "So, Ishaan, out of these three ladies that I mention, you have to chose who would you kill, marry, or hook up with? The names are: Deepika Padukone, Meera Tiwari and Priyanka."

Ishaan laughed at her question and replied after taking a moment, "I would marry Deepika, hook up with Priyanka and then since she is the only one left..." He looked at Meera, who was looking at him angrily and continued, "...I'll have to murder Meera."

Meera retorted like a little school kid, "I don't want to play this game. No one takes my name. *Chalo,* marriage is too serious. But Ishaan, we could have hooked up at least?"

Kavya looked at her sister with horrendous eyes. '*What is this idiot saying? I am sure she doesn't even know what hook up means.*'

Pretty obviously, Ishaan also thought the same. He had some hundred awkward expressions dancing on his face. He, however, guessed that Meera wasn't too sure what hooking up meant.

But, Meera was Meera. As if saying this for once wasn't enough, she reiterated it, "Ishaan, we could just hook up, right?"

'*Shit, this idiot!*' Kavya thought and kept her hand on her face, trying to hide her smirk that Ishaan captured and asked, "Kavya, *bachpan me isko Horlicks nahi pilaya tha kya?*"

Then, he turned to Meera and said, "I am sorry yaar. We will hook up some other day. Let us all sleep now."

And saying so, Kavya showed Ishaan his room. Both of them laughed and laughed more. Ishaan just said, "Good night, *baccha*."

That was the first time he called her that and she was touched. She didn't say anything, but smiled genuinely at him and gave him a warm hug. Brother, sister, friends – these relationships aren't made by counting days, but they are built on the immediate connect you feel with someone. Yes, it grows as time nurtures it, but as they say, the building stone is the first step to build a strong structure.

While some relations need time to grow, Ishaan and Kavya were lucky to have that trust built on the very first meeting. None of the three could define their relation, but Meera knew one thing – Ishaan and Kavya shared an immediate connect, which she always wanted to stay!

She could just see two different people in them when they were together, especially Ishaan – she saw his smile, forgetting all the mature thoughts that he had, forgetting his responsibilities, work and pressure – he was just himself. Meera loved his smile.

She could see both of them so elated together – it was just bliss!

♦

"You are such an idiot, didi," Kavya said as she entered the room.

Meera looked at her with puzzled expressions.

Kavya asked, "What does hooking up mean?"

"What kind of a stupid question is this, Kavu? It's not something a tenth standard kiddie should know." Meera replied, being the nerdy elder sister.

Kavya retorted, "Yes, sure. But, it is something a twenty-two-year-old should definitely know. You are too embarrassing, *yaar di.*" Kavya laughed and then asked again, "Tell me no, what's hooking up for you?"

Meera replied, just wanting to go to sleep. "It means going on a date, right? Like just the two of you and a lot of talking."

Kavya laughed louder and she almost fell on the bed laughing. Meera was still puzzled. She asked, "What's wrong with you?"

Kavya just laughed, realising that her sister was too innocent to understand the sexual connotation behind the words. She just hugged Meera and said, "*Bhaiya* was right. You needed more Horlicks as a kid."

Saying so, the two sisters slept. The day was too eventful for them, wasn't it? While Meera probably was a supporting cast for the day, it was all about a new relationship – Kavya and Ishaan. As much as their interests matched, Kavya loved the way he pampered her, and he loved pampering his younger sister.

Some relations are too fond of each other to be understood by the eyes of world.

"Meera, you are the best!"

Sleeping in a new place, Ishaan was distracted. At 4 a.m., he woke up to sip some water when he realised that there was some sound that was echoing.

He tried to concentrate on the sound. It was a uniform sound of the keyboard. It would be consistent for while, then would stop for a minute, then, it would again be loud. At this time of the night, he expected neither Meera, nor Kavya to be up. After all, they had slept close to 1.30 a.m. And being extremely sure of this fact made him a little scared of the sound.

'*Meera would never get up at this time – she's a princess, she would be sleeping cosily in her luxurious round bed; neither would Kavu get up. Who is it then?*' he thought.

However, gathering some courage, he got up and opened the door of the guest room. Thanks to Bollywood, he was scared and a little apprehensive. He had also seen *Fear Files* and *CID*, note that too. Ishaan, the epitome of calm, was scared and a little clumsy as he walked towards the drawing room, only to find Meera.

Sitting cross-legged on the carpet of her drawing room, Meera was extremely focussed and was looking at her laptop, without even blinking once. She was diligently taking notes and was maintaining a diary of the same. With her round-framed spectacles on her face, she looked like a complete nerd. The focus on her face brightened Ishaan's eyes for a moment. He was amused by the fact that Meera always was exactly the opposite of how he had judged her to be. When he thought she would react maturely, she always did the opposite by messing things up; and when he thought she would be '*Papa ki pari*', she proved him wrong with her hardwork.

He couldn't help but admire her at that moment. '*We slept so late and even then, she is up and working at 4. Perhaps, this is what people call dedication.*'

It was a good morning, he told himself. He then walked towards the kitchen, without disturbing Meera, and switched on the stove to make tea for the two of them.

Somehow, he didn't feel the awkwardness of a new location at Meera's place. He felt a strange level of comfort. He went ahead and made tea. While pouring it in the cup, he smiled at the thought of Meera being Meera. '*She's just a new packet of surprise everyday!*'

He wasn't someone who would show gestures like these for anyone, but somehow Meera's ambition forced him to care for her. There was something which completely sloshed him in her – it was her passion, maybe; or her attitude; or her innocence; or her madness. He always used to say, *it is good to not know why you like spending time with someone, because then you'll spend more time in order to know why you like being together. It's a win-win situation.*

◆

As he walked towards Meera, he stole a glance of the hardwork that was evidently visible on her face. As he took a step towards her, his heart made a knock on his brain. Looking at her calm, his heart had a volcanic eruption and feelings poured out naturally.

His heart so desperately wanted to tell him what it felt, but Ishaan being Ishaan, ignored what his little heart had to tell him. '*The heart is immature. Keep it away,*' he repeated to himself as he took the next step towards her.

As he walked nearer to her, his heartbeat was much more evident to his ears. While the sun was rising that wintery morning, his heart too was getting up from the cold space that he had forced it to stay in. And when the heart starts to rebel, mature or immature, it usually wins.

He smiled and sat next to Meera, who was sleepy, yet she made efforts to complete what she was writing. She was startled when she saw him standing next to her with two cups of tea. Every morning when she got up, she was habitual of making tea for herself. Seeing someone else make that effort for her was a little awkward for her.

She asked, a little zoned out in her work, "Hey, you needed something?"

She was just about to get up when Ishaan kept the tea mugs on the table and pushed her down by her shoulders on the ground, saying, "Good morning, Miss Blogger."

Meera smiled and in her ever so charming voice, she replied, "Good morning, Ishaan."

He sat next to her on the ground when she said, "Hey, pull a bean bag, no."

He simply gave her an assuring smile, saying, "You work every morning?"

Meera nodded, still working on the document and replied, "Give me five minutes. I need to complete this reading before I close my laptop. I am sorry..."

"Shh. Work. I'll be comfortable," he replied, tapping on her palm assuring her that he could wait.

In that moment, there was nothing, but there were too many things. In those five minutes when he stayed quiet and she worked, there was nothing that she noticed, but there was a life that he saw in her focus. He had never seen her more confident and diligent, and looking at her passion for her dream, all he could feel was proud. So much so that when she closed the lid of her laptop, the first thing he said was, "I know I am going to start with a serious talk right in the morning, but consider me as your friend or well wisher or senior, whatever you feel like, and hear what I have to say."

Meera sipped from the tea cup and exclaimed, "I love this. You are a good *chaiwala*." He smiled gently. She continued, "And, why are you getting all this serious right in the morning?"

He replied, concerned and much serious, "See, you are getting what you want at a very early age because you've worked hard for it. All I really want to say is that with this success comes more responsibility and that responsibility demands more stability. I am being very straight in saying this, but I hope you will understand my intentions behind this..." He continued and Meera heard him in the pin drop silence of the room.

Never had any friend tried telling this to her, she thought at the back of her head.

"Keep calm and don't lose your patience out of excitement. Life demands you to be a much calmer person than you are in the profession you want to make your career in. Don't let these small milestones change what big is coming your way. I don't know if you understand what I mean – but, I just want to tell you that I really really wish that you get what you aim for in your life. I want your fashion blog to be India's best."

As she heard him speak for two continuous minutes, she simply smiled when he paused. Never had she seen him talk so much and when she did hear him speak, it was nothing less than a pleasant surprise. She never thought he would notice all of it about her and she never had a friend who cared so much about her work; or perhaps she never noticed any care before.

"*Ek baat bolun aapko?*" she asked, looking at him innocently.

"*Haan.* You felt bad about what I said, right?" he asked, apprehensive.

He never gave such *gyan* to any of his friends. He always thought that people had their own lives and they were capable enough of taking good care of themselves. Therefore, he never intervened in anyone's lives, but somehow he felt like talking to her about what he felt about her life, about her decisions! He was ignoring his heart, but it still thudded, right? And since this was the first time he said what he actually felt like, he was hell nervous of the reaction he would get. Meera could see that nervousness.

She replied, putting her palms over his. "Aren't you too conscious about yourself, Ishaan?" He smiled sheepishly as she continued, "You know what? This is something only a real friend will tell me. See, most people I meet will appreciate me for my blog, my presence on social media and on the events I go to as a motivational speaker, but what no one will correct me on is – what you just said. I am happy that you said what you did. I am always gonna keep this in my mind, I promise."

She gave her hand that he held immediately and one promise was made while the sun rose in the sky to brighten the cold morning.

Perhaps this friendship was also like the sun rays in the cold winters of Delhi – every person in our life is for a reason and there is a reason for everyone to be the way they are. But, you know there are a few people you like being with, you like talking to, without any reason. And my metro buddy always said that when you have no reason to be with someone, that is when you should actually stay there. A lot of times, what he said became a learning for a lifetime.

Ishaan and Meera had no reason to be with each other, but slowly and steadily, they liked each other's company, they enjoyed being with each other and they loved dreaming. This morning just materialised this fact to the two of them individually – accepting the fact or not, was again, a personal choice!

Half Mental Full Crack

Have you ever seen how a scorpion camouflages himself to protect himself from predator? That's exactly how you have to adapt to some situations at workplace so that the frustration just flows through and you can survive the situation. And trust me, be it school, college, office or business; no particular phase would continue for an endless time. It always changes. It does!

What didn't work out today, will work tomorrow. If you've failed in an exam today, you'll pass it tomorrow. What's such a big deal? What's important is to keep going!

The relationship between Meera and her supervisor was deteriorating day by day at her workplace. They would have cold glances, incomplete conversations and awkwardness, which was visible to everyone. Their team knew of their equation, their colleagues provoked Meera to share what was wrong between them, and the lead managers could also sense friction.

They could see Meera's angst and her trouble to cope up with the situation. There are always good and some not so god people at work. Some care for you, some don't. The best way to fare forward is to admire those who care for you, and ignore the ones who don't.

Her managers could see what was visible to them – that their workplace had friction. But, what no one was able to see was the friction that was building up inside Meera. Her frustration was destroying her peace. And no, the frustration was not because she had a mean supervisor, but because she wasn't able to manage her blog because her mind was pre-occupied with the politics that was going on around her.

Yes, she was a positive person, but when there is a constant negative ambience around you, you start getting affected. She would not feel like going to office, she would think when would it be 5 and she could leave, she would regret the fact that she was spending more efforts in office than she should give to her work. She just wanted to get rid of the vicious cycle she was getting stuck in.

While not everyone could see her deteriorating positivity, Ishaan could. In just fifteen days, he could read what was going on in her life.

'*She hardly smiles these days. It's always either silence or cribbing. It is affecting her personality,*' he thought as he looked at her while they sat together and had tea. He knew exactly how the workplace environment could suppress dreams and when he saw such potential in a dream, he just could not let anything affect Meera's dream to build a worldwide fashion blog.

'*Her skeleton wasn't built to follow a 9 to 5 routine. She is meant to fly freely. I can't look at her stupid silence,*' he told himself.

He refused to accept the fact that Meera's dreams could step down in her priority list and that very moment, the person who wasn't even ambitious for himself was extremely ambitious for her. He promised himself to stay by her side for reasons not even known to him.

◆

"So, how's your blog going?" he asked, as they sat in the cafeteria.

"Forget it, Ishaan! Not this topic," Meera replied, evidently annoyed.

"And why not this topic?" he asked.

"Because I don't want to talk to anyone about anything," she snapped.

Had it been anyone else, Ishaan would have given up, saying 'what do I have to do. Your problem, you resolve', but because it was her, he reacted differently. He took out his phone and recording her reaction, he asked again, "No, tell me, why don't you want to discuss your blog? Let your fans also know this."

Meera had a tear in her eyes and wiping it, she smiled at his innocence. She kept her palm in front of her face and exclaimed, "Have you lost it? You can't make a video just like that."

He smiled, looking at her smile. '*Finally, she at least smiled.*' "And you think you can just walk away from a family of readers and friends who want to read about what you think about fashion, just like that?"

As he spoke, she had another tear dropping down from her eyes, looking at which, Ishaan sat next to her and wrapping his arms around her shoulders, said, "See Meera, when your work demands you to be like a twenty-six-year-old, why behave like someone who is eighteen? Balance your work."

As he was explaining this to her, he picked up the tea cup and made her take a sip from it. *Hold on, statue! Both of you, I wanted to say.*

In the breezy weather, sitting on the roof-top cafeteria, that moment was worth capturing when Ishaan and Meera sat next to each other and he held her so lovingly. He continued, "Just act a little mature, Meera. Reduce the stress of your office issues and do not let it affect your work. Remember, that is your work."

Meera smiled broadly. As he looked at her smile, he reiterated to himself, '*The way she is, she just needs to focus more on her work. Rest, she knows her work best. I'll be that friend who stays by her side whenever she needs me.'*

Was it a promise for her, or was it a promise that he wanted to make to himself, he wasn't sure; but what he was extremely sure of was the fact that he really wanted to be right there – to see her blog flourish.

♦

As they boarded the metro, Ishaan took out his earphone, switched on some peppy songs and acted indifferent. Meera wondered what had happened to him suddenly. *'He was all talkative when we came here. What happened to him now?'*

She patted his back, when he removed his earphones and asked, "What?"

Meera was taken aback. *'Who behaves like this?'* she thought and asked, "I am sitting here, you should talk to me."

He replied, "You are sitting here, you should write. We've spoken enough for the day."

He waited for her to take her laptop out, but when she was still arguing, Ishaan took out her laptop, switched it on and then, inserted his earphone in his ears again, deliberately ignoring her.

Touch wood is all that I would say, looking at the moment. As the metro ran, so did Meera's fingers on her laptop's keypad and she wrote one of the most engaging blogs. As she was about to leave, Ishaan said, removing his earphone, "You are a genius at work, but you know what?"

Keeping her laptop inside the bag, she asked, "What?"

"You are half mental full crack."

Meera laughed for a while and then getting up and leaving, she said, "School's over, Mr. Ishaan."

"That's what I am trying to tell you, Miss Blogger."

And in between laughter and some quirky conversation, the half mental full crack... I mean Meera left for her place and happily enough, she was up at 4 a.m. to work for her blog.

'Let's get married for a day, Ishaan.'

Next morning, when Meera wrapped her work, she called Ishaan at 6 a.m. He was still sleeping and got up only looking at the screen of his phone.

"Goood morning, Ishaan!" Meera exclaimed, full of enthusiasm.

"As much as I appreciate your energy right in the morning, you realise I am still sleeping?" he replied.

"So, get up! We'll go together in the metro today onwards," she said.

"Oh no – weren't evenings enough for you to trouble me?" He smirked. In his heart, he knew he would have a blast when she travelled with him, but if he expressed what he felt, how would he still be Ishaan?

Meera laughed and kept the phone. She got ready in a pair of casual jeans and wore an off white shrug over it. She applied some dark lip shade and kept her hair wavy and open. Quickly, she applied some kohl and eye liner. And once she was done, she looked in the mirror and could see the older Meera back. '*I had been going to office like a zombie since these two weeks. Today will be a good day.'*

The conversations with Ishaan were making her go back to the original self that she was – where nothing else but her own blog mattered.

◆

As Meera was running and reaching ten minutes late, Ishaan was happily waiting for her in front of the sixth coach, third gate. She reached and said, "You wait for me every time. You are so sweet, Ishaan."

"What is wrong with you? Have you taken vodka shots right in the morning?" he asked.

If her original energy was that of '*dhinchaak*' Bollywood songs, for him, the morning was silent, soulful. He had never seen someone this energetic right in the morning.

As they stood in between the crowd, Meera held his bag. That was typical of her – whenever she was afraid to lose connect with someone, she would hold them tightly. For the first time, she was afraid of losing his company.

And as soon as they entered a crowded metro, she said, "Ishaan! I want to get married for one day."

He was amused and so were the people in the metro who heard this girl talk so loudly, right in the morning. Her voice was so loud that it was also audible to someone standing in the next compartment.

"Sure, go ahead!" was all that he said, knowing she was in her 'high' mode.

"So, you agree to get married to me for a day? We'll have so much fun... food, clothes, dance..."

By this time, everyone around them was enjoying the conversation. Ishaan knew this and considering that everyone was looking at them, he kept his hand on her shoulders and said, "Meera, let's talk about this later."

"Of course not! Please say yes. See, you are sweet, you know me so well, you wait for me, you care so much. Had I not been so much against marriage, we could have had it for a longer time, but for now, one day, would be fun," she tried selling her idea.

Ishaan looked at her with an unbelievably disgusted look. He had never been the centre of attention in an over-crowded metro, but then, he had also never been with someone like Meera.

He was quiet, hearing her nonsense but at the same time, he was happy that at least her positivity was back. Meera kept going on...

"On second thoughts, you and I make a good couple. Imagine – glitter, bangles, nail paints..."

Ishaan interrupted her and said, "This is why you wanted to travel with me in the morning?"

Saying so, he opened her laptop, held it in his hands and then said, "Enough of the kiddish banter. Work now."

As she saw him hold her laptop for her to work, she said, "It's a crowded metro, and my laptop is heavy. Your hands would hurt."

"Shh. Meera, work!"

And as the metro reached their destination, Meera was already on a journey to her destiny. She didn't know who Ishaan was for her, but her commitment-phobic personality could see an enemy in Ishaan for sure.

On the other hand, he could tolerate everything – all her childish fantasies if that helped her come on track with her blog. A friendship like none other and feelings like never before – both of them had too many different emotions at one time.

♦

As they sat in the cab towards their office, Ishaan asked, "Why are you so negative towards marriage?"

"Because I feel that marriage pulls you away from your dream," she replied.

"I know that feelings make us week. But, trust me, once there is the ultimate person you can spend time with, this insecurity of yours would just disappear," he tried to explain.

"Nonsense! Relationships take the ambition away from you. And, I can't afford to distance the only thing that keeps me going," she said, being evidently adamant.

Ishaan was surprised and slightly disappointed with what she felt about love and marriages. He perhaps did not expect her to be scared of love – it was him, who was scared of feelings, but for her, he didn't know why, but her adamant answer perturbed him a bit.

And with that thought, they reached office. The day was much better when Meera hardly paid any heed to her supervisor's taunts. What mattered for her was the fact that she was a genius, yet 'half mental full crack'.

'Sometimes, just listen to the one walking with you.'

"Ishaan, have you heard about *Manyawar*?" Meera asked him as they were talking over phone later that night.

"Yes. That's a wedding clothing brand, right?" he asked, diligently listening to what she said.

"That's right. They have sent a collaboration request to promote their brand," Meera replied.

"What would that mean?" Ishaan asked.

"It would mean that I would write stories on marriages, functions and festivities for the next month, subtly promoting their brand," she explained.

"That's a good deal, I believe," he asked.

"Of course! It is way too much work starting today, Ishaan. But, I am all the more excited to begin this huge project," she said.

As the clock turned to 1 a.m., Ishaan smiled to himself, hearing her non-stop banter. *'She has stories for almost everything. And she speaks so much. And, what's strangest is that I love listening to her.'*

As his mind had this confidential conversation, he said, "Go and sleep now. You also have to get up at 4."

Meera behaved like a kid when he behaved like a teacher.

"It's okay. I will anyway get up," she retorted.

"If you don't want to go alone tomorrow morning, go and sleep. Otherwise, I am not coming with you," he said, strictly.

Meera made a face and then slept, happily enough with the new assignment that she had just received.

♦

The chilly winters of Delhi had started to make way for spring and as spring started to arrive, some brightness began entering Meera's life as well. She was working devotedly towards the new project.

Every day, she would leave office with Ishaan. They would take the metro together and every day, he would push her to write. Every day, she would be miffed with something or the other, and every day, he would pacify her angst in the cab by making her most comfortable. He perhaps was the only person Meera had built a strong trust for in her office.

There are some people who you can trust without any apprehensions. Ishaan was that person for Meera. His calm, his maturity, his strengths and his unsaid weaknesses – she accepted them all. They travelled together in the mornings and evenings. In fact, it wouldn't be wrong if I said that their days started and ended with each other.

Just the other day, in one of their journeys back home, Ishaan was standing right at the corner of the platform, much ahead of the yellow line, when Meera simply held him by his elbows and pulled him back. Ishaan was startled to feel her hand around his, when he immediately turned towards her.

(So, for those who aren't familiar with Delhi metro, the most crowded metro starts from Huda City Centre, Gurgaon and to grab a seat, you have to have some super powers because, a seat in the Delhi metro is precious, trust me.)

Ishaan and Meera stood amidst a swarm of crowd, but their eyes refused to move from each other's. As Ishaan looked straight in her eyes, he found admiration and when she looked back, she found care. As the two of them stood in front of each other, their hearts thudded again – loudly, this time and this time, both of them could hear the heartbeats clearly.

They were inches away from each other and their hearts finally were happy to hear each other speak the language of expressions. As Meera's grip on his hand tightened, the next metro too passed from the platform. The crowd changed, the metros passed, but one thing that didn't change was Ishaan and Meera. For that moment, life existed in those feelings for them and in the next moment, they distracted themselves smartly.

Ishaan, who was extremely uncomfortable inviting feelings between them acted indifferent and said, "You scared the shit out of me."

Meera, who was equally uncomfortable in committing to feelings, replied, "You know the metro officials have taken deep trouble in painting this yellow line. It is not to be crossed."

"Whatever!" he said and once again stepped on the same yellow line.

'*Stubborn,*' she registered and gave him a disgusted look.

'*Cranky,*' he noted. But, to add to the adjective, Meera declared, "I won't take the metro till you come a step back."

"Shut up, Meera! All my life I've boarded metros safely. Stop being a teacher," he argued vehemently.

"Teacher or no teacher – we won't board the next metro till you step back," she argued.

The situation that looked breezy and romantic a minute ago

was funny now. The two of them arguing and the crowd was once again a spectator. The scene was interesting and it reached its climax when the metro arrived.

Ishaan said, "I am leaving. And we won't get a seat if you don't come with me."

"I don't care," she said and stood firm to her words.

'*Immature*,' he called her for the first time in his mind. He was able to get a seat for himself, sitting from where he called out, "Meera, I am sorry. I promise I won't ever step ahead of that line. Can you now come inside?"

In these thirty seconds, they had the smallest fight ever that ended with Meera entering the metro and standing on the side glass near the gate. Looking at her standing, he got up as well, leaving the biggest possession of his life for the first time – a metro seat. He couldn't imagine he had left a metro seat for someone.

He stood in front of her, near the glass on the opposite side and smiled at her innocence.

Meera said, "Why are you standing here, how about going to the next coach instead?"

He read the sarcasm and walked near her. He didn't say anything but looked at her. Silence was a companion for the next ten minutes, after which, he explained, "See, I am sorry. But, sometimes, realise that I have my own set of ways. You might have your own…"

As he was speaking, Meera kept her palm on his mouth, concluding this miniature fight, "Sometimes, you can listen to the person with you. Sometimes, life is just that simple."

Once again, unsaid concern wrapped in the leaves of stubbornness won and the hearts that were thudding aloud were silenced. Once again, Ishaan and Meera won over their feelings for each other, and once again, the journey took them a step closer to each other.

Is this love?

Ishaan wrote to Meera.

> Hey HMFC.

> What on earth is this HMFC, Ishaan?

> Half Mental Full Crack. Remember I named you that day?

Meera, who was lying lazily in her bed at 10 on a summery Sunday, just gave him a disgusted emoji.

He then asked,

> How's the response to the new project on your blog?

> It is good. Yes, there is a lot more that can be done to the blog, but it's doing pretty well for now.

I just felt like telling you that not everyone can dream as freely as you do. So, just love that fact and dream more.

What's up with you, Ishaan? So philosophical right in the morning?

Morning for me is at 5 and you know it!

While Ishaan was watching some news channel, lying on the sofa in their living room, he thought, '*I don't know what it is. I am not able to decipher the language in which my heart talks to me these days. I don't know why, I try my level best to make her feel comfortable and I have no clue as to why I always go beyond being myself to make her smile. She is a kid, she is immature, she is full of life, she is cheerful, but she, at the end of the day, needs to get realistic. I know all these facts, yet I want to be with her.*'

Over-thinking! And perhaps for the first time for him. Ishaan wanted to stay away from it. And the only person he liked talking to, when he felt lost was Kavya. He called her and after their general chit chats, he said, "Kavu, there is something that is troubling me."

"What's that?" Kavya asked casually.

She was the most chilled out person. Even when there would be a house on fire, she would first finish her Netflix series and then bother to go and ask if everything was fine.

"Your sister," Ishaan said, not knowing if he should say so.

"Haan, she is irritating and *chep*, I know," she replied.

Ishaan laughed for a while. Sometimes, Kavya's ignorance

to problems just inspired him to do exactly the same. He knew only she could bring him out of his over-thinking mode.

"What did Meera do this time?" Kavya asked.

"She didn't do anything. But, I just feel that she gets distracted too easily. As in, if someone would ever want to enter her life, he would not, thinking that she isn't mature enough to deal with two things at a time. She is brilliant with her work, but I just feel she lacks that focus..."

Kavya heard what Ishaan said quietly. She was surprised that Ishaan had to say so much and had done so much analysis on her sister. "Bhaiya, it's okay. She has been that way and that's how she has always achieved what she wanted. What's the problem then?" Kavya said.

"The problem is that her dreams are bigger than anyone else's," Ishaan said.

In his mind, even he didn't know what the problem was, but something, somewhere was troubling him. While talking to her, he was perhaps trying to find out what he was feeling wrong in her, because technically, it was nothing.

Kavya replied, "Don't worry bhaiya. I know Meera – she messes things up, but she is strong enough to bring that mess to a sorted scene. Trust me, if not her."

And as Kavya kept the phone, Ishaan wondered if he was actually over thinking and if Meera could actually manage everything herself. Just then, his brain had to intervene.

'All I know is that her dreams are something bigger than what a common man dreams and it needs her attention and dedication. How can someone even think of entering that space? I think only her writing can tolerate her tantrums.

'Plus, she is a commitment-phobic – just like I am. How do you expect her to understand what you are and what you wish from your life?' he thought.

As he looked at his television screen that blinked headlines and video shots, his mind wandered in the farthest of islands. And while he was thinking about the complexity of the situation, Meera was already complicating it in her mind.

Just to understand the situation better, Kavya asked Meera, "How's Ishaan Bhaiya?"

The reply was, "He is the calmest person I've met, Kavu. His calm just pacifies my vigour every day. I just can't believe that I have someone who pushes me to write every day; to comfort me of my office stress…"

Kavya smirked at the fact that she knew something was brewing somewhere. She just interrupted her, saying, "Bro, you need help. I just asked if he was fine or not. That too pretty casually. Well, I am really sorry that I did. I'll ask him myself."

Saying so, Kavya took her phone and left the room, leaving a question revolving in her sister's mind, *Actually! Why am I going overboard by telling everyone about how wonderful Ishaan is? What is happening to me?* Thinking so, she just took the remote of her AC and switched it on, keeping her thoughts away; or should I say, running away from them. She slept again, thinking that sleep would help simplify the situation.

Truly, if one was ocean, the other was fire. If one was emotion, the other was a stone. Together or not together, they were friends. This fact perhaps was the one that kept them bonded.

♦

Standing amidst the crowd once again, standing in front of each other and looking straight into each other's eyes, it seemed as if the earth was rotating around the sun, the planets were revolving around the sun, the plants kept pumping oxygen to the world and the world kept moving at its own pace but, two hearts stopped.

Once again, the metro arrived and once again everything was the way it always was, except two people – Ishaan and Meera. They stood inches away from each other and once again, they were able to hear the hearts beatings and the sound of each other's breath.

As she heard his heartbeat, her heart skipped a beat. As she could feel his aroma, her senses gave in, as she looked at his face, she tried her best but couldn't ignore his eyes, which never received her attention. And in that moment, his lips looked so innocent, just as if they were waiting for someone to make them break into a smile.

At that moment, her fear towards commitment, her loss for expressions and her disability to feel feelings – all collapsed in front of him. At that moment, only *he* mattered.

Meera took a step forward and looking straight into his eyes, she was just about to meet his lips, when she felt a push. And with that push, the scariest dream of her life came to an end. Kavya was standing right there, asking her sister to get up. She threw a pillow at Meera and shouted, "Di, you've been sleeping for ages. Get up now!"

And Kavya left the room, leaving behind Meera, who was baffled with what she had seen. *'Damn, what was my mind doing to me? Ishaan – what was all that I saw?'*

She closed her eyes and once again saw what she was just dreaming of, when she immediately opened her eyes. She kept her palms on her face and cribbing of what she had just seen, she went to the washroom and splashed some cold water on her face, trying her best to take herself out of what she had just seen.

'What the fuck is wrong with me. How can I think about all

*of this when I have my own blog to set up? Plus, Ishaan? Shit!
What am I thinking?*

'*Maybe I just need to reduce the time I am spending with
him. Maybe, I need to focus a bit on my work. I need to be more
focussed.*'

The chain of her thoughts ran throughout her mind just
when Ishaan called.

"Hey Miss Blogger, do you want to go for ice skating
today?" he asked.

'*Say no. You need to create a distance. Relations pull you
back...*' Her mind started to instruct her when she answered,
"Sure. I'll see you at Ambience Mall in an hour or so?" her lips
said.

In her mind, she knew how much he loved adventure and for
the first time, Meera thought about someone else before herself.
She knew that she would have the hangover of that dream, but
she still wanted to face reality.

◆

As they reached and took their skates, Ishaan quickly got his feet
in the heavy skates, while Meera struggled. She wasn't able to
put the skates properly and was getting irritated by the fact that
she wasn't able to wear them on. She was as cranky as a baby
at times.

Looking at this, Ishaan sat down on the floor and held her
feet, putting the skates properly.

As he sat down and diligently put the buckle of the skates,
Meera tried her best to not notice him. But she couldn't stop
herself from feelings what she had been trying to ignore. Result
of her conflicting mind was a tear drop that sparkled from her
eyes. And, even in the dimly-lit skating area, with the cold breeze
of dry ice and the dampness of the atmosphere, Ishaan could

catch that tear before she wiped it off. He asked, concerned, "Meera, what's wrong?"

Sitting **next** to her, he didn't know what had happened in just a minute.

Meera, on the other hand, just asked her mind to shut up and hid herself in Ishaan's embrace. She held him tightly and hid her face in his calmness. He was startled and disturbed both – startled by the closeness and disturbed by the same.

'*She needs to handle her emotions herself. I will not be with her forever,*' his mind told him.

"Meera, what happened?" His lips asked, embracing her hair in the most caressing manner.

How could she tell him that he was the reason behind her mind's conflict? How could she tell him that even when he was the reason she was chasing her dreams so well, he was also the reason behind her mind's fight with her heart.

She just wiped her tears, separated herself from him and said, "Nothing. Just one of those bad mood swings. Come, let us go!" she said and gave him her hand to get up.

He held her palm as they went to skate. As always, Ishaan was flowing through one corner to the other and looking at his happiness, Meera was elated. On the other hand, she struggled to walk step by step. She had now started to walk without any support, but needed some caution.

However, whenever they came for ice skating, it was never her joy; in fact, she always had pain after wearing the heavy skates, but she never said it out loud. She was always joyous seeing Ishaan be a kid once again. She tried talking to him several times about his life, but he always chose not talking about his choices, his decisions and his life. He was always silent and was forever ready to hear what she had to say.

'*He is always eager to hear what everyone has to say. It is lovely to see him enjoy where he wants to, for a change,*' she thought, taking baby steps.

And just when she was walking slowly, Ishaan came swaying and asked, "All good?"

Meera smiled broadly and said, "Absolutely. I was just trying to walk independently."

Holding her hands and taking her to the middle of the skating rink, Ishaan said, "You already are independent. You just need to believe this fact." Saying so, even when they were in full speed, he left her hand and went away, leaving her all to herself and swaying as happily as he did. Undoubtedly, he was right – Meera did not fall. Rather, she enjoyed the moment.

She was happy and cheerful and looking at her, all Ishaan told himself was, '*Meera is someone who is capable of achieving so much. Just that her feelings need to be in control of her. Right now, her emotions drive her.*'

And with that, the day ended for the two of them with a happy dinner and conversations that were never ending. But one thing that had seeped inside their friendship was feelings.

Would the two of them sail through the dicey boat of emotions and feelings was a question worth asking, though. What do you think – Is this love?

6th Coach 3rd Gate

Next morning, amidst confused feelings and annoying expressions, Meera and Ishaan were all set to walk ahead. Which way, they did not know!

As Meera rushed through the crowd of Rajiv Chowk towards the yellow line, she could see Ishaan waiting. He was fiddling with his phone, the way he always did to pass time, and was standing peacefully in a corner. To her, he looked extremely cute at that moment.

'*Thrity-five minutes, and still he never complains. This guy is just another level,*' she told herself, once again, complimenting his simplicity.

As she rushed and met him, she said, "I am so sorry…"

Just then the metro arrived and Ishaan said, "Come on, quick!"

Whenever they travelled together, he would always meet her in the sixth coach, in front of the third gate. This was only on days when Meera was on time, which by the way was rare. However, whenever she entered the metro and saw him, her eyes breathed a breath of relaxation. Sometimes, she wondered how drastically her metro journeys had changed. Being a student of Delhi University, she travelled everyday and loved being alone, talking in soliloquies – she loved her solo trips, unlike now, when she was in love with the journey itself. She enjoyed his bad jokes, his smile, his sarcasm, the way he scolded her, the way she irritated him, the way she deliberately flirted with him. The person and the ambition was the same, but her expectations from life had changed.

As they got inside the metro, Meera stood inches away from him, holding her laptop bag and looking up into his eyes. She said, "You are a really nice person…"

He interrupted her genuine words and said bluntly, "If it is your flirt mode, not right now, Meera."

For once, she felt bad and went silent for a while, noticing which, Ishaan asked, "So, you won't smile? And won't even look at me?"

There wasn't any reaction.

"Yes, you shouldn't definitely talk to me. *Bilkul mat karna.*"

A little smile jumped on her face and hiding that, she said, "You can't do this. Let me be angry. I don't want to laugh right now; don't force me to."

"Of course not, Meera! I would never want to do that. I don't want people around to be scared," he said and in just a fraction of seconds, her smile was back.

She said, smiling this time, "I joke, I know. But, this time I was serious. I appreciate your patience."

He looked at her. He wanted to tell her that her presence too was appreciated deeply by his heart, but just said, looking outside the windows of the metro, "This patience has helped me a lot, Meera. And therefore, I want you to imbibe it as well."

Meera asked, "Yes, I will, when the time comes. I am happy being myself right now."

'*Even when it is kiddish?*' he questioned. In his mind, but said out loud, "Not every time will you find me with you. Just remember to be patient with situations. Not every time will you have a person waiting for you. At that time, wait and be patient with yourself."

Meera saw seriousness and when she saw him in this mode, she generally didn't interrupt. However, just because she was in a light mood today, she nodded and then, asked, "Ishaan, tell me one thing – were you a photographer?"

He kept quiet, knowing for sure that this would be a lame joke.

"Tell me no, do you like clicking pictures?" she insisted.

"Meera!" He gave her the Ishaan look, ignoring which, she asked yet again, "No, tell me."

"Yes, I like clicking photographs," he said, succumbing to her stubborn wishes. She wouldn't say a single word till she got her answer.

But, as soon as he replied, a smile blossomed on her face. She completed her sentence, saying, "I knew it! Because I start smiling whenever I look at you."

Disclaimer: Never use any pick up line that Meera uses. It might be injurious to your relationship.

Ishaan looked at her in shock for a second. And then laughed loudly. That seriousness vanished and Meera felt relaxed. She desperately wanted the seriousness between them to go away and when it did, she enjoyed their togetherness all over again.

"From where do you get such ideas, Meera?" he asked.

"As you always say, *apna apna* talent *hai*," she replied, quoting him.

They were about to reach their destination, and Meera was facing some irritation in her eyes. She complained of itching and pain in her right eye, when Ishaan quickly said, "Let's get down at Huda and we'll get some eye drop from the medical store at Fortis Hospital."

Fortis was just opposite to Huda geographically. Meera nodded and by the time they reached the pharmacy, Ishaan had already searched for the eye drop. He asked the guy at the counter, "FML 10 ml."

Taking the drops and paying the pharmacist, Ishaan also booked a cab for the two of them. I must admit that when he cared, he cared a lot. He, born a Sagittarius, would never express but sometimes, his gestures gave words to his feelings.

Walking towards Meera, who was extremely cranky by now, he helped her sit in the cab. Handing the eye drops to her, he said, "Just put these and your eye should be fine."

Meera took the packet, quickly opened the eye drop and in a jiffy, tried putting the drops in her eyes. She wasn't able to put the drops in her eyes even once, result of which the drops fell on her cheek.

One, she was irritated. Two, she wanted to get rid of the irritation, and three, she was extremely cranky. Ishaan looked at her and patiently waited for her to put the eye drops.

"Ishaan, take this eye drop and put it in my right eye!" She almost ordered.

He had been thinking of helping her since the last four minutes, but he feared coming close to her. And now, thanks to her highness and her tantrums, he wasn't left with a choice. Smiling at her innocence, he took the eye drops from her hand and shifting towards his left, closer to her, he hesitantly held her head from his left hand, careful enough of not hurting her. He pushed her hair behind her ears and cleared her forehead.

His soft hands had some strange impact on her. Immediately, all her crankiness vanished and her heart calmed itself down automatically. He came a little closer to her as he dropped the liquid from the eye drop in her right eye. That moment was worth capturing when Ishaan and Meera were inches away from each other – he caressing her and was extremely careful while handling her and she, adorably looking at him, feeling every bit of the moment . Ironically, both of them felt ticklish inside their hearts when they were so close, but none of the two would let feelings enter their mind, result of which, they expressed nothing and reached office.

Ishaan ensured that her eyes were fine throughout the day and that she didn't strain them a lot. Undoubtedly, he cared. But, undoubtedly, for him, it was just care. As a friend, he cared for a friend, he reassured himself.

With these two, it was more of running away from the feeling we commonly call love.

But, even the sixth coach, third gate of the metro knew that what it witnessed every day wasn't just friendship. It saw trust building, it saw apprehensions changing to assurance, it saw some said, some unsaid emotions and it saw Ishaan and Meera being there for each other. The only difference was that Meera never said she was there, but no matter what happened, she stood by him. On the other hand, Ishaan felt he was just solving her problems.

There were complications that had started building up in his mind, even when he tried his best to keep them away. There were feelings which did their job and there were emotions, which he never welcomed in his life. And being himself, he wanted to run away from the two most complicated words to simplify his life – feelings and emotions.

'It's a dream, not a back up, Ishaan'

"She is a bubble of positivity to her team, an asset to the managers, and someone who has worked endlessly throughout the wavy journey. She is none other than Meera Tiwari," the anchor of the awards ceremony announced.

Like every other corporate firm, Apticon too had their awards for each month. And after working day and night for her new project, tolerating her supervisor's taunts and tantrums, finally Meera had proven her mettle to the management. She had received the title of a 'Silent Superstar', along with the Star performer for the month of May.

She walked gracefully and took the award, acknowledging the appreciation, and in her mind, Ishaan's support. But, one person who wasn't affected was Ishaan. Rather, he was unhappy when she got the award.

In the cab that day, he said, "Good that you got an award. Congratulations! But, I am sorry, I don't see it as something you deserve."

Meera was puzzled. This was the same person who was always pushing her to not put her papers down when she most wanted to keep them. And now, when she had finally started getting the recognition, he wasn't even appreciating it.

"Ishaan, as much as I try, I don't get you at times," she said, a little annoyed.

"You won't. I am different with different people. And, it's impossible to decode me," he replied rudely.

Sometimes his mood swings were a tad bit difficult to handle, and Meera's way of dealing with such situations was that she just ignored the moment and kept quiet. Experiencing the worst of getting in an argument, she preferred keeping quiet when he was miffed on reasons unknown to her, which were many, by the way.

And she knew, when she would keep mum, there would be awkwardness in the cab and then he himself would speak. She trusted him to fill in that void, and he never let her down. This didn't change even this time. He said, "You deserve the awards for your blog. I know working hard is your forte and you are by default a hard worker, but I just don't want this to affect your work as a fashion blogger."

Meera looked at him silently, as he continued, "The company recognises you because you work for them. But, that doesn't mean you'll start keeping them above your dreams, Meera…"

For the first time, she understood the reason behind his rudeness and knowing what he was feeling; Meera respected him all the more. She kept her palm on his and reassuring him, she said, "I am not keeping the corporate life above my dreams, Ishaan. That is a promise."

Her confidence definitely calmed his mind, which had a turmoil going on inside it. The spark in her eyes when she spoke about her dream was sufficient to bring the turmoil in his mind to a standstill.

"Meera, I know you. You work on your blog because the kick for you is to get out of this place. Once you get comfortable here, you won't..."

He was talking, when Meera interrupted him, "You say, understanding you is a task, but do you realise how little you know about me?"

She looked at him and there was pin drop silence in the cab.

"I work because I like working here, I am learning something new and I am gaining some experience – not just in work, but also in life. See, handling Sadhna gave me the confidence of dealing with such situations, right? I am here in the company because I like my work, but my blog – that is a dream I want to live. So, I am just working to build that dream."

He heard her peacefully. Calming him down, she tapped on his palm, explaining, "The blog I work on is not just another hobby of mine that I consider as a back up to the 9 to 5 job. It is my dream. Trust me, it is not a back up. It is the only ambition I have in life. So, nothing matters in comparison to it." She continued, "It really isn't about a back up and if you call it so, I think you are being unfair to my dream. It is humiliating for my dream to be called a back up."

As she said so, he realised how passionately in love she was with her aims. At that moment, he realised that blogging and writing wasn't just a dream one teenager saw, it was her life and the only reason that gave her inspiration to go ahead and work more.

'*She deserves to achieve all her dreams, without any distraction*,' he told himself and they entered the metro. Unlike every day, it was Meera who took her laptop out and started working.

Even when there wasn't any space to sit, Ishaan ensured Meera got a seat and protecting her laptop, he just stood in front of her, covering her from the crowd.

For once, Meera looked at him and respected his presence in her life.

For once, Ishaan looked at her and respected the presence of her dreams in his life. She inspired him to work more, to achieve more, to dream more.

Once again, it was a DSLR moment when she wrote dedicatedly and he stood, no matter how tired or exhausted he was – ensuring she was writing. Feelings never make way just like that. They always have logic and a reason and those who say feelings happen to those who aren't logical, they are undoubtedly wrong, my friend!

Every emotion, every feeling and even one-sided feelings enter when they are allowed to enter. To say that they were assumed or mistaken is just a masquerade to cover the inability to accept them.

♦

Evening after evening, as they travelled together, they were collecting memories, moments and stories. As their work started complimenting their potential, Meera and Ishaan both were enjoying their togetherness. Of course, both of them had their inhibitions, apprehensions and moody zones, but the best part was that both of them could handle all of this with each other, for each other.

And, amidst the quest between confronting and escaping the feelings, even Delhi's summers came to a haul. In between the humidity of the city, the showers of rain came as a blessing. And being the first shower of the year, the water droplets so beautifully cleared the dust on the green leaves, making them look greener and healthier. The earth rejoiced with the nourishment and Meera's heart jumped with excitement.

First, it was her birthday month and being herself, she was extremely excited for her birthday.

Ishaan messaged her to leave at 5. She looked outside the window.

> Ishaan, it is so beautiful outside.

> Of course, it is. But, we need to leave. I am booking the cab. See me in 5 minutes at the gate.

As much as small things excited her, he was indifferent towards them.

Being himself, he was quietly waiting for her and the cab driver, when the whole world was enjoying the first rain showers.

'What's wrong with people? They need to grow up,' he thought as he saw everyone around him enjoying the blissful showers.

For him, it was a usual day and for Meera, he was the most unusual creature on earth. She just looked at his lack of excitement and thought, *'Even if I try my best, he'll never be excited about anything. He's just khadoos.'*

As the cab started, she commented, "If there were awards for being serious, trust me, you would win the most number of those."

Ishaan just gave her his patent, 'I am not interested in your banter' look and asked the driver, as he always did, "Bhaiya, radio?"

Meera punched him on his shoulder and dramatically said, "You have such a beautiful girl talking to you and you want the radio."

He smirked. Meera hit him on his shoulder again and said, "I am hungry and…"

Just when she was about to make demands of junk food, Ishaan took out a blue box from his bag that had *mathris*. He opened it for her and said, "This is all that you get today. We aren't stopping at Huda to feed you today. I am getting late."

Meera was just about to make a face, when Ishaan took a piece of mathri and landed it right in her mouth. He knew taste was the key to her brain. And he was sure about the taste this time.

"Wow. This is so good. Give the box to me," she said, enthusiastically taking the box from his hand.

Ishaan smiled at her innocence. At times, this innocence transferred her naïve positivity in him. He said, looking adorably at her, "Mom made these and I kept it because I knew I had a kid travelling with me."

She smiled and said, "I want to talk to your mom."

"And why would you want to do that?" he asked.

"Just like that," she replied, still eating. "Actually, I want to visit your home this weekend," she added, confidently.

Ishaan looked at her with weird expressions. "I wonder at times, how hopeful you are. I am neither taking you home, nor calling mom right now."

Meera kept quiet. Just then, the cab stopped at the metro station, where the cabs, autos and cars were enraging a war against each other. There was water, traffic and trouble. The cab driver instructed, "Sir, *jaldi utarna, warna jam badh jaega.*"

The Sir in the cab got the instruction clearly, but when Ishaan got down and looked back at Meera, he saw her sitting inside the cab with a smirk.

"Meera, get down. Quick!"

The cab driver was equally disgusted and worried, knowing

he would have a *chalan* if this mad girl didn't get down. The traffic, the rains, the pleading Ishaan standing in the rain, the disgusted driver – nothing mattered to the girl sitting comfortably on the back seat of the Wagon R. She simply said, "Promise me that you'll take me home this weekend."

"What in this world is wrong with you, Meera?" he shouted, as the rain drops fell heavily on his face.

The cab driver intervened and said, "Madam, please."

Meera smiled at him and said, "Sorry bhaiya."

Ishaan, getting miffed, said, "Okay, fine. I am leaving."

"Bye," she said, sure of the fact that he wouldn't leave without her. "This tactic was my mum's favourite one and I never gave into it," she added as she saw him come back and that too, with a smile.

He said, "Okay, I'll take you home this Saturday. Come, now."

He extended his hand that she held immediately and jumped down the cab, just to realise that she was wearing her brand new shoes. As they walked towards the gates, she saw a pool of water, to which, she told Ishaan, "Ishaaaan!"

Whenever she spoke in that tone, he knew there was something that was coming up.

"Hmm?" He looked at her.

"I am wearing the new Vans shoes. I don't want them to get mudded with the water there," she said.

Ishaan kept walking and replied, "I thought shoes were supposed to get dirty anyway?" As they walked, he added, "How does it even matter?"

"It does. I love these. And Kavya gifted these to me," she replied, genuinely. This time it was no tantrum or *zidd*, but a genuine request that he saw in her eyes. So much so, that he agreed to find a different way for her.

'*Yes, you are the Creator, no? Find a way now.*' His mind poked him as he held her wrist and told her, "Just walk with me. No cribbing about the distance now."

Meera smiled and entwining her fingers in his, agreed. With the drizzle around, the brightness in the dark and the nurturing nature, Meera found her inspiration, perhaps. She was quiet and just followed his footsteps to reach the platforms, where Ishaan said, "Your shoes are sparkling. Perks of being with an engineer, haan?"

Meera smiled and realised that taking the untaken roads, figuring out dry stones and taking the pain to walk the whole road with her, he ensured that her shoes were still new. And this no longer was about those shoes. It was about the care, concern and love! Meera smiled broadly at him and hopping back to reality, she reminded him, "I am coming home on Saturday. Tell this to everyone. It will be fun meeting them."

He knew arguing was just a waste of time with her and he knew that her visit would be an entertaining one for everyone at his place. Especially, when she would be the first ever guest that he would take home. He could imagine the expression on his mother's face when he would tell her.

It was difficult to invite a guest at home and it was extremely difficult for someone who never liked guests at home. Ishaan never liked anyone coming home – never, but when Meera insisted, he wasn't irritated about it.

Strangely true, but true!

Ye tera ghar, ye mera ghar!

"Hello aunty," she said with a bright smile on her face as she touched her feet.

Ishaan's mom was an extremely lovely lady. Meera saw her and exclaimed in her mind, '*Aunty looks younger than me. She is so adorable.*'

Typical of Meera – she would always love people admirably. Impulsive, she was. At the same time, his mother was equally elated to see an enthusiastic young mind at home. With two boys around, she hardly got to hear such a cheerful voice. Imagine, Ishaan being cheerful? (I know you are already smirking, just at the thought of it.)

His mother welcomed Meera warmly and while Meera enjoyed the pampering, he silently sat in one corner with tired expressions. He always wanted to escape awkwardness and therefore, he never welcomed anyone to his place. However, he couldn't even walk away, considering it was Meera and it was extremely important to supervise what she spoke, because she spoke without any filters. Knowing this, he couldn't take any risks.

"Beta, tell me one thing honestly," Ishaan's mom asked.

Meera was listening carefully and hearing this question, Ishaan too got alert. Otherwise, he was busy fiddling with his mobile phone.

"Yes, aunty?" she asked.

"You self-invited yourself, right? Because, knowing my son, he would never invite anyone."

Ishaan gave an angry frown to his mother, noticing which, Meera jumped in the conversation, "*Haan ji.* I thought I'd love to meet the person who cooks the best *daal ke paranthe* ever and he straight away refused to bring me home. So, I tried to convince him for inviting me."

Ishaan smiled, remembering how eventful her way of convincing was!

Laughing and talking, aunty replied, "I am glad that you came over to meet. At least I got someone to talk to, otherwise he just comes back from work and goes off to sleep."

This sounds so much like a melodramatic Rajshree movie sequence, I know, and I am trying hard to keep it real, but kya karien, Meera herself is a dramatic human and so are situations related to her.

Meera looked at Ishaan, who was making faces, hearing his praises.

Aunty added, "But, the paranthas you love aren't cooked by me, dear."

Ishaan interrupted, "Let's have lunch, mom."

Meera held aunty's hand and asked, "Aunty, wait! Who cooks them then?"

Aunty smiled and got up, saying, "The most silent person in my house."

Meera exclaimed, as she followed his mother inside the kitchen like Mary's little lamb. "Ishaan?"

Aunty nodded. "He gets up early and helps me with the chores before he leaves for office. He certainly is the best son one could get," his mom said proudly.

Meera smiled, listening to what aunty had said. Once again, respect towards him doubled in her heart. In that moment, he was the definition of perfect for her. He was a perfect son, a perfect brother, a perfect colleague and a perfect partner, she thought.

She had seen his quiet side, she had also seen his talkative side, she had seen his anger, she had also seen his ignorance and she knew his will power – yet, in that moment, she felt that she still had a lot to know about him. He was right, he was different with different people!

◆

"Oh wow aunty, you have a wonderful music system," Meera said, as she sat at the dining table, waiting for lunch.

"Yes. That's my companion when I take lunch alone. Plus, I like Bollywood songs."

Meera smiled as she sat for lunch and aunty served her with the most delicious dishes she had prepared. As she served her, Meera was overwhelmed by the love his mother had served in her plate. The plate was not only filled with food, but also with love and admiration. It had rajma, rice, dahi vada, kheer, jeera aloo and lacchha paranthas. Aunty said, "Have the kheer! If you loved the paranthas, the same chef made the kheer also."

Meera looked up at Ishaan, who was sitting in front of her. Meanwhile, the radio had the song, *Rashke Qamar* playing on it and for the first time, the lyrics of that song touched Meera's heart. Once again, there was something in the atmosphere. What it was, she didn't know, but something that her heart was registering again and again. Maybe, it was respect for him, maybe it was admiration, maybe attraction, or maybe – love?

◆

As they walked upstairs to the terrace of his place, Meera was mesmerised. She stood at the brim of the terrace, looking at a picturesque side of Old Delhi. A Gurudwara stood just in front of them and the breeze blew calmly. Incidentally, it was drizzling when they stood on his terrace and looked at the beautiful scenery.

For the first time, silence felt beautiful to Meera, but it felt burdening to Ishaan. He broke the silence that was building feelings between them and asked her, "What's the one thing in life you really want?"

Meera didn't argue this time, but just looked at him and said, "To be India's fashion icon."

As she looked at him, her long hair came between his and her eyes, but couldn't disrupt the eye lock between their eyes. Even the drizzle wasn't able to break their speaking eyes.

He asked, "If you have to sacrifice the closest things that you own, even then you would choose your blog, right?"

"Yes," she replied immediately with a spark in her eyes.

"And what if you fell in love with someone?" he asked, not being himself but being truthful to his heart for the first time.

"Even then, priorities don't change. Plus, I think, I can't afford to be in a relationship," she replied and just in that moment, he decided, '*Yes, she can't afford to lose her focus.*'

'*Plus, she'll never understand what commitment is. She is immature to understand what true love is. I think it was I who was wrong in expecting maturity from her. All she can do is joke about her one-day wedding.*'

And just in that moment, something crashed. They did not know what it really was, but something changed for sure. Just in that moment, when everything was more than beautiful, it seemed as if something stopped. That moment was lovely in itself – Meera was busy finding how much she respected him and he was busy analysing what his heart told his brain! Just in that little moment, two different ideologies were playing together – about the same thing, but in two different directions.

None of them knew what changed, but something certainly did!

'What's wrong
with you, Ishaan?'

Just like every day, Meera messaged Ishaan just as she got up.

> Good morning Mr. Tom. See you at Rajiv Chowk at 7:20. Sixth coach, third gate.

She smiled and got up to get ready while Ishaan read the message and unread it from his mind. He simply replied, unlike every day.

> Leave. I will come late.

When Meera was all set to leave her place, she read his reply and could feel a strange disconnect. Weird it is, but true, that messages express every emotion, may be not through words, but through the gap between those words.

She called him immediately and looking at her number, he looked at his phone uncomfortably. Till the time it kept ringing, his heart and brain kept fighting – one wanted to talk to her, like it did every day, and the other wanted to get rid of solving problems for a kid.

Ultimately, this time the mind won and he didn't pick up the call.

Meera was annoyed and messaged him.

> What's wrong?

He didn't reply. Meera was sure by now that something certainly was wrong and being herself, she called him again. Those thirty seconds when her name flashed on his screen, he was disturbed. And once again, he didn't pick her call.

'*Let her solve her own problems now. It's high time she does that.*' He reiterated to himself, trying to convince his heart why he shouldn't pick her phone call.

On the other hand, Meera was extremely disturbed throughout the day. She messaged him on Skype, on mail, on text and on WhatsApp, but he didn't respond to even one of those. Meera was upset throughout the day. The cafeteria, the Skype chat, the mails – nothing seemed to distract her from the constant fact that Ishaan had stopped talking to her – *just like that*.

For her, there was a deep void that was filling her insides. Slowly, the silence that Ishaan was serving her became a web that she wasn't able to escape. It seemed as if with each passing minute, one string of that web was captivating her; reiterating to her that something, somewhere was wrong. The ambience in office seemed burdening and therefore, dropping a message to him, she left at 4.

> I am sure you wouldn't want to come along. I am leaving. Bye.

As he read the message, he was satisfied.

'It will take her a week, but she'd be fine. The bond between us isn't such that it wouldn't fade easily. If we don't talk for a few days, both of us will get used to not having the other one around.'

His reply to her was short.

K.

The most irritating reply in the whole world, by god. It irritated her immensely. She messaged, evidently angry.

> You know what, Ishaan? When I behave with people in a certain way, there is a reason behind it. But, I have never behaved the way you are behaving with me. At least tell me what's wrong? I have the right to know why we aren't talking anymore, right.

As he received and read the message immediately, his heart wrenched and told him a hundred times to tell her that it wasn't anything but the fear of falling in love, losing her ambitions and his focus. He so wanted to tell her that she was a great person and her innocence could brighten any gloomy morning, but ended up replying later that evening, while travelling alone.

> Don't follow me if you really want to talk to me. I am irritated and therefore, stop bugging me with your name on my screen.

She received that message when she was lying on her bed, thinking about what went wrong. The message disturbed her further.

And why are you irritated?

You will know the reason when I feel you should.

'*What's wrong with him?*' Meera asked herself and replied, sternly.

When friendship starts to have an 'I', you know friendship is no longer the same.

He didn't reply.

'*She and her taunts would end soon, I am sure,*' he thought.

He wasn't sure if he could let her go so easily, but he was sure that staying there wouldn't work for either of the two. For him, at his age, he looked forward to a serious relationship, which she wouldn't ever be able to accept. He faced the same anguish and the same pain of walking alone, but he had a motive clear in his head – her dream. He knew somewhere in his heart that he needed her, but his brain directed him in exactly the opposite direction.

'*Feelings make you weak. And they just can't enter your life right now, Ishaan. She is immature, she won't understand,*' he told himself.

Immature – perhaps this word became the easiest excuse he had to not only pacify her questions, but his heart too. And then, people say – you start believing what you constantly tell yourself. Ishaan was doing exactly the same thing.

On the other hand, Meera had fat tears dropping down her eyes.

And why did you get irritated all of a sudden?

Her intuition said whatever he was doing wasn't really himself but reality just presented everything in a haphazard manner.

> It was never all of a sudden. It had been happening for all these months and I always told that to you, but it was you who assumed that I was kidding.

He replied and switched his phone off, even before he could see her reply.

This perhaps was the start of escapism for him. In the dilemma between the heart and the mind, the mind won. In the competition between his happiness and her career, he consciously chose her career; in the competition between their companionship and his focus, he wanted to live with his focus; and in all of this, he just concluded the chapter by telling himself that he was too busy now to solve problems for someone who was a kid. He thought that saying so was enough for Meera's ego to be hurt and for her to move on.

'It's a crush that she has on me. It'll end as soon as we stop talking. How long lived are such feelings, anyway?' He was convinced.

If this is what he assumed, he hardly knew her.

For Meera, life was what she wanted to build, and for her, if love had happened, she would do her best to build the castle of her love story with the cement of her ambitions.

Ignorance was his weapon to kill their feelings. If he was using it as a knife to brutally murder her feelings, her dedication towards her friendship was her shield to protect whatever existed between the two of them. In between this war, there were bruises, bloodshed of emotions and impending pain. Just the fact that either both of them would win, or both of them would lose.

With each wry expression they shared at workplace, Meera's cheerfulness died a silent death. She was breaking piece by piece just by the fact that he wasn't talking to her and that too, without having any reason.

'*How could he just walk out of my life like this?*' She kept wondering and then, there was silence. No conversation, no words and nothing existed between them till they started for Ranchi.

And, when I say, 'nothing', it just doesn't include the sleepless nights both of them went through, the frequent breakdowns she went through and the void that two hearts had at the same time. Both of them knew what feelings were, both of them knew how feelings worked and how they were running away from them.

THE NEW BEGINNING

I Love You

Ranchi was like a dream that Meera had lived. The silence somehow started to disperse and conversations had started building in. However, as they landed in Delhi, reality once again welcomed her with a jerk.

As much as she was hopeful of their togetherness, Ishaan was sure of the distance he wanted to build between the two of them. Yes, both of them were stubborn – Ishaan in maintaining and eventually increasing the distance that he had built, and Meera in putting in every effort to reduce that distance.

When you walk with someone and then suddenly that place is vacant, you feel the jerk more strongly. As they returned from Ranchi, Meera was once again pulled back to every memory that gave her everything back then, but today, all that those memories could give her was pain and tears.

Their cab conversations, his lamest jokes that made her smile, his calmness, the messages on Skype, their video calls, the way he scolded her on small things, the way she got upset on the smallest issues, the way he managed to motivate her and the way the two of them had started to walk together on that journey – every little thing became all the more important to her. All of a sudden, nothing remained 'theirs'.

As she stood in the queue for swiping her metro card, she remembered how he had mocked her once, saying she always chose the longest line.

'*Paagal hai tu!*' echoed in her head as she walked alone towards the escalators. Every day, she would find him waiting for her below the escalator, and today, when she walked and habitually looked at the corner, it was vacant.

Once again, like the past few months, reality pinched Meera hard. Like she was still throwing herself back to the time which had stopped in July. As she climbed the escalator, she looked at the staircase on the right. As she took a step forward towards that staircase, she remembered how she held the handle of his bag and raced to the top. Today, no one was there to compete with, she told herself, and walked like a zombie – silently, wiping a tear from her eye and trying to be strong.

And then, as she reached the platform, she remembered all their arguments on standing behind the yellow line and the banter that followed. And, by the time she sat in the corner-most seat of the metro, she knew that she couldn't keep these memories buried inside her heart. At that moment, she knew she couldn't let her feelings die a death without even expressing them. He existed in every second of her life; how could she let him go without even telling him how important he was?

In Ranchi, nothing was fine, yet it looked stable. Even when they didn't speak, the world kept revolving, because at least they were together. Meera was still fine with silence when they were together. But, once again, the void of being alone was something that was pulling her down.

'*If it has to end, I at least need to tell him what I feel,*' she told herself and taking out her phone, she wrote:

I know you might not even read this, but I wouldn't be able to live with the regret that I never expressed the truest feelings I ever felt for someone. And since you decided we won't talk ever, here's what I felt from the day we stopped talking.

Ishaan, I love you and these feelings were something I never felt when we were together. Jab baat karna band kar diya, tab se *I know what you mean to me. Each day, I was clearer about my feelings, which I wasn't earlier. In these six months of silence, every second my heart spoke to me and told me how important your presence was for it.*

That's when I knew that feelings weren't a joke. And, just wanted to tell you that for the first time in my entire life, being commitment phobic also could not help in keeping my heart away from you. Till the time we were together, nothing mattered, but every second after that silence has ensured me how much you matter to me. I really thought I could spend the rest of my life with you.

Never was I ever sure of this decision as I was with you, Ishaan. I always ran from it till I thought about you! I wanted to be beside you forever.

And not because I want you to solve my problems or because I need you – I just like being with you. I wanted to be someone you could share what you want with.

I never wanted to interfere in your space.

Even if you are a roller coaster, I thought I could handle the roller coaster mood swings that you had! Till we spoke, I never realised my feelings, and now, I am so sure of their existence that I'll not want to let them go! We talk or we don't, I'll keep them safe!

However, this is what I feel. Trust me, I don't expect anything in return. I realised ki jab *feelings* nahi thi, *expectations* thi *and* abb sirf *feelings hai* toh *I have learnt to let go. If it's meant to be, it will.*

I really like you and more than that, I respect you for being what you are!

Lastly, I know that at this moment, for both of us, career is the first priority and that's what should define us, but I couldn't keep these feelings inside anymore.

I just want this to be the happiest memories and I don't want myself to be the memory that irritates you, so will quietly take a step away now on. Now onwards, you wouldn't need to escape from a kid, the kid will walk away graciously; and that's a promise.

You are someone I look up to being like! Thank you for being the inspiration for my writing and sorry for being kiddish. I think I know now that it is irritating!

That's all!

Bye'

And, as she pressed the sent button, her heart thudded loudly. There was some burden from her heart that had just found a vent and as she saw the message received, her heart skipped a beat.

'*What would he feel after reading this?*' she asked herself as she got down from the metro and made her way home.

◆

Just in the next metro was Ishaan, who was being forced by his emotions to go back and remember the same things, the same place where he would wait for her, the chats they had, the conversations where he spoke, unlikely of himself, and each little thing that was present then and had disappeared now. He missed her company, but couldn't embrace those feelings and ended up ignoring them.

It was as if he was aware that he was being affected, but he did not want to accept that fact. And, just as he unlocked his phone, he saw the long message Meera had written.

Reading the four words, '*I Love you, Ishaan*', he closed his eyes and felt the emotions with which she had written those words. For any other person, these words would have just mesmerised you inside out. And to an extent, Ishaan was no different. He couldn't hide a smile and the feeling of hearing the most awaited three words. Of course, he loved her too.

But, just then, it was as if reality came in front of him and focusing on himself, he read the rest of the message putting a lock on his heart.

'*What a kid. Who says all this?*' his brain told his heart.

'*And, why did she have to send this?*'

'Why *did I have to read this? I should have deleted it even before I read it,*' his mind constantly told him as the metro paved its way.

Ishaan switched off his phone, switched it on the next minute, deleted that message and then, out of anger, blocked Meera.

Yes, he was angry with her for expressing what she felt. He was annoyed with her because he thought that she assumed his care as love. He was upset because he was hurting one of his closest friends and he was fiercely anxious because he didn't know how to handle himself, forget handling the situation. And in all of this, blocking her was the easiest option available, no?

Once and for all, he won't have to see her.

◆

Meera entered home and saw that there wasn't any display picture on his WhatsApp account. It took her exactly a minute to realise that Ishaan had apparently blocked her, not only from WhatsApp, but from his life as well and that realisation wasn't a glorious one. She simply went inside and sat on her bed, in front of Kavya, and broke down into tears.

Kavya, sitting in front of her sister knew what she was going through, even when she didn't speak anything. At that moment, knowing both Ishaan and Meera, she was angry at the situation.

'*Why do people have to be in a situation where everything has to be messed up?*' she questioned, looking at her elder sister, who she had never seen the way she did today. For Kavya, Meera was the epitome of strength, who never broke down; no matter what. Looking at the transformation, she was annoyed at the situation and just went ahead and hugged her sister.

Hugging Kavya tightly, Meera cried harder, saying, "Kavu, I love him. I really do."

Kavya replied, not knowing what else to say, "I can see that. But, that is okay."

"When people on my Facebook page send irritating messages, I block them. And today, I got blocked by someone..." And Meera broke down again.

Kavya stroked her hair and said, "Di, I always tell you that if it is meant to be, it will happen; else nothing would matter. Stop crying!"

And saying so, she quickly brought dinner for her sister. Even when Meera made faces and threw tantrums, Kavya made her eat a chapatti. When she went to keep the plate inside the kitchen, Meera opened her phone, saw the blank profile picture and felt everything at the same time: anger, hatred, love, helplessness, and most of all – pain.

She was an independent blogger, someone who was renowned and had never faced rejection ever in her life. Forget love, she hated commitment. Being all of that, she had expressed what she felt.

Can you imagine what Meera was going through? Someone who was a commitment-phobic gathered up the guts to express what she really felt. Through these years, she never fell in love because that was never her zone, and today, she just proved herself right. Love wasn't meant for her.

His blocking her just broke everything – her self-respect, her confidence, her passion and most importantly, her heart.

'*He could have just explained that he did not feel the way that I did for him. Why did he have to insult me?*' Sobbing and over-thinking, she finally fell asleep.

As Kavya came inside, she saw her sister being in the most vulnerable state, the way she had never seen her. Stroking her hair and holding her hand, she wondered why were the two people she admired the most in such a situation.

'*How will Di perform in her event day after,*' she questioned as she saw her elder sister sleep.

Meera had a motivational lecture in one of the renowned lit-fests on fashion blogging and it was the first time she would be living what she had always dreamt of. But, looking at her right now, not only Kavya but anyone would be doubtful of her session.

Maybe, when it's meant to be, it will; if not, never.

'Dreams do come true, Meera!'

"Kavya, get ready in five! We have to leave for the event," Meera told Kavya, getting ready herself.

Kavya smiled at her and not being sympathetic deliberately, she said, "I take two minutes to look awesome, unlike your hundred minutes. And wait – even after that, you look boring."

Walking towards Meera, she applied some lipstick to go with the pink one piece dress her sister was wearing and made her change her boring earrings to some fancy ones, saying, "Now, you look like a celebrity."

Meera smiled as the sisters left for the event. But, as soon as they sat in the cab, Meera took out her phone and called Ishaan. For some strange reason, she hoped that everything could at least become the way it was. Maybe she was living in a world which had nothing left except for her hopes. She called him twice and he didn't pick up both the times. A tear dropped down her eyes, wiping which, she entered the Lit-fest, which was gigantic.

As they got down the car and mentioned that she was the speaker, they were escorted till the hall, where the organisers met Meera, greeted her and treated her as someone who was of extreme importance. For a minute, her self-doubt was thrown away; for the whole session, her endless thoughts about her nature being immature were brushed off, and she was living the dream that she always wanted to.

The name on the 'Speaker's card' she wore around her neck, the name on the speakers' list, the ambience and the reality that was the start to her journey of achieving her dreams – everything made her a little proud of the hardwork she had done in the past five years. Yes, that getting up at 4, the endless thoughts and the uncountable hours of work were finally yielding success, and more than Meera, her sister was proud of her.

Kavya took a little video of her sister speaking from the stage, with confidence and strength sparkling through her eyes and posted it on Instagram, where she wrote,

'Proud of my sister – who is an epitome of strength for me. My inspiration.'

And within a minute, Ishaan replied, 'Even I am proud of her.'

Kavya sent him a smiley as he asked, 'How is she?'

For a second, Kavya didn't feel like replying, but she did, considering Ishaan wasn't wrong either, and she loved both of them equally.

'Right now, on the stage, talking about her journey.'

She sent a few pictures of the event, when Ishaan smiled broadly and replied, 'She is meant for the stage. All her attention should be for her work and no one else.'

Kavya wrote, 'Yes, her work keeps her going, no matter what.'

'I hope that this stays forever.' He wrote and their conversation ended.

Meera walked down the stage with grace and an aura that defined her as a successful fashion blogger. She wasn't looking vulnerable, nor did she look disappointed. In fact, she lived those moments because those were the ones she had wished since a very long time.

Even Meera realised the fact that her work was the only boat that could sail her through the phase that she was stuck in. As she walked down the stage, she knew her work was the only backup that she could fall back on. And being herself, she just didn't want to let go of the opportunities that were coming her way.

And on that note, she came back and worked on her blog, endlessly. *Kehte hai na,* you just need hope to sustain, and with her, perhaps she was too hopeful!

'Get a hold of yourself, Meera.'

Every day, Meera wouldn't sleep on time, but get up at sharp 4. She would work endlessly and then leave for office – alone. She would try her best to keep her spirits high in the morning, retelling herself that her worth was far more than just being accustomed to loving someone. And every day, by evening, she would fall less on energy, she would struggle to survive with the feeling of loneliness and she wouldn't fail in failing herself every single day.

That feeling of failing yourself each and every moment of the day – that kills you inside out, especially when you know your worth is much beyond what you are limiting yourself to.

When you disappoint no one else, but yourself; when you trouble no one else, but yourself; and when you demean nobody but the self sitting quietly inside you. Every day, Meera wanted to set her priorities right, but she failed to implement. Every day, she would tell herself that she had to move on, but she would inevitably fail at it. Every moment, she assured herself of her dignity and then, every other moment, she tried contacting him and broke that dignity in her own eyes.

Unrequited love never fails you; it is you who fails yourself. How was it Ishaan's fault if she had taken a vow to disappoint herself? How was it anyone else's responsibility if she had vowed to fall in her eyes? How was anyone else to blame if she was the one wanting to ruin herself?

And while Ishaan made every possible effort to not even see her, the real fact was that they were in the same office, under the same roof, and there were moments when they crossed each other. One such day was when Meera had come up to the cafeteria with one of her team mates and so had Ishaan.

When she saw him, she walked towards him and asked, "I wanted to talk to you."

He did not reply and kept eating his snacks.

"Ishaan," Meera repeated, confidently this time.

"What?" he replied, with some extremely obnoxious expressions and with this expression, her confidence was again shattered.

"I need to talk to..." she tried repeating, when he said, "You are just being irritating. I said I don't want to talk to you."

She already had a lump in her throat, but she still gathered words to face the insult she was facing.

"Why? I should at least know..." her words were not even audible. Her eyes looked humiliated with insult and her face looked grim.

'*Why Meera, please don't make me do all of this. Why do you have to be so stubborn? Just accept that I am a jerk and give me a tight slap,*' he thought as he behaved like the most idiotic person to her. He knew he was being mean and he knew it was important, because otherwise, she would never give up on him.

He just got up and said, "You are such a stalker. Okay, I'll leave."

Meera had tears flowing down her eyes, when she looked

down, held his wrist and said, "No. You won't go anywhere. Stay!"

"I will leave," she said and ran downstairs, leaving her colleague behind. Meanwhile, Ishaan couldn't finish his food. He threw it and as he walked out with the rudest face possible, his heart too wept. Silently, of course.

As he left office, he felt sick of himself. He felt exceptionally villainous doing all this to the person who he cared for till a month back.

'*What am I doing? I know she would break down after this. Still...*' he thought.

'*But, this would then become her last effort. I know her ego; she won't call me after this, hence ending the chain of pain for her as well. This is good for her,*' he continued thinking.

As he took the metro, he received a text message from Meera.

We'll never meet again. That's a promise.

Reading that message, he felt bad, he felt gloomy and he felt weak. You know, Meera's love was visible enough – she knew about it, he also knew about it and her reactions were evidently visible. However, Ishaan's love, if it existed, was silent. He was trying hard not to know it, he tried his level best to not tell her and he had mastered the art of not expressing it. In between this difference, imagine how would he feel?

He wasn't wrong, he wasn't mean, but was pretending to be. He wanted the best for her, but he had ensured she hated him. Imagine how he would feel when he knew in his heart that he was right, but he couldn't even tell it to her. Even when he pretended to be extremely strong, he was equally vulnerable at that moment. The only thing that he kept telling himself was that he did not love her.

If that made him feel better...

'It's okay to let yourself free, Ishaan!'

'A Sagittarius may not talk to you anymore, but they'll always love you the same.' He posted as his WhatsApp status.

His WhatsApp status too had the liberty to know what his heart felt, but he had just restricted himself so much that he didn't even let his heart breathe.

Every morning when he got up to leave for office, he was devoid of cheer. It wasn't that he did not miss the time they spent together – he missed it and the worst part with him was that he did not even express it. He hated disrespecting her, but yet he did. He had started being someone you would not want to go and talk to. He would speak what was important.

His eyes had endless apprehensions and just when he tried to move away from her, she called him. In the spurt of the moment, he picked it up.

"What?" he said, rudely.

Whenever Meera called, he would want to ask her how she

was, how everything with her was. But, ended up just saying one word, every time.

"Ishaan, I forgot my wallet today. Would it be possible for you to lend me a few hundred bucks for today? I'll return..."

'*Of course,*' he thought of replying, but didn't.

'*This is just a way to talk and reduce the distance from Meera. I will not let this happen. In fact, I know how egoistic she is. Let me refuse to give any money,*' he told himself.

"No. I don't have any money."

"PayTm?" she asked.

"I said no. Keep the phone now."

Once again, there were tears in Meera's eyes and there was guilt in his heart. He very well knew the fact that Meera was someone who wouldn't ask for money until it was extremely important. He felt bad doing what he did, but he knew he could not even give her any hope. He was bent on reducing any chance that they could meet.

♦

"Meera, is everything okay at home? You look extremely worried since a few days," Meera's supervisor asked, genuinely concerned.

Imagine a supervisor as harsh as Sadhna could also see her pain. Meera hardly spoke to anyone, hardly made efforts to gel with others or to uplift her mood. It was as if she had accepted that she wouldn't smile. All she focussed on was her blog and that definitely gave her solace.

To her supervisor, she said, "No, everything is perfectly fine, ma'am. Don't worry."

Sadhna smiled, knowing what she got as an answer was outrightly a lie. She then asked, "Did you have lunch?"

It was 4 p.m. by then and these days, she never saw Meera

away from her system. She just stared at the desktop and focussed only on her work.

"Yes, I had some fruits and Maggi a while ago," Meera told her and appreciated the concern Sadhna had towards her, and once again, started to look at her system till it was 5.

At 5, Meera wasn't feeling too well. She felt like giving a call to Ishaan, but remembering what had happened a few hours back, she did not call him. Rather, she picked her bag and booked a cab.

Even when she was in the cab, she felt uncomfortable and dizzy, but she pushed herself to reach Huda City Centre. Meanwhile, she messaged Kavya.

Kavu, I'll reach by 7. Not too well.

Kavya immediately replied, considering her sister's health in recent days.

Where are you, di?

Huda Metro.

And as she walked towards the metro station, her head was spinning and it seemed to her that Huda City Centre was rotating in front of her eyes. Her knees were feeling extremely weak and her head wasn't stabilising. Even now, she felt like calling Ishaan, but she didn't.

Call it self-respect or foolishness, she was stubborn on not calling him, even when she needed him the most. She somehow gathered her strength and tried walking ahead.

She would have walked exactly four steps towards the entrance of the metro station when she could no longer keep her head in its place. It was spinning at a speed that even she couldn't decipher and in less than a second, she lost control of her body. She tried holding onto the wall, but in the next minute, it seemed as if the wall too had started moving to her and she lost her grip to that wall too.

In the blink of the eyes, a girl, wearing a little black corporate dress, was lying on the floor of the metro station, unconscious and alone. She literally had no sense of where she was and just fell on the ground with her bag clinging to her shoulders, and her phone lying in the lose grip of her fist. As the crowd gathered around her, one of them poured water on her face, trying to bring her back to consciousness.

Someone from the crowd tapped on her face and asked, "What's the password of your phone? We need to call someone."

Meera did not reply. She wasn't in any condition to reply. But, fortunately the person who was handling her phone tried the emergency contact, which could be dialled even without the password.

He called the number which was on her phone's emergency contact.

The voice from the other end said, "What?"

The guy said, "Hi, whoever is the owner of the phone has fallen down at Huda City Centre. Yours was the number in her emergency contact and hence I called you."

Ishaan was taken aback. He replied, hassled, "Thank you. Please stay there, I am coming." He rushed towards the metro station.

He reached Huda in less than fifteen minutes and ran towards Meera. He knew how he spent those fifteen minutes away from her, in guilt, in regret, in looking back, in pain. Meanwhile, she had gained some consciousness, but was too weak to get up.

As Ishaan reached the metro station and saw her sitting on

the bench, he simply ran towards her and seeing her, he just embraced her in a tight hug.

She, who was still dizzy, could feel him, and in that moment, could feel all the emotions she was craving for. As Meera felt the strength from within when she felt she was in his embrace, experiencing every emotion that she had been desperately waiting for. She felt joyous, rejoiced would be a better word. As she felt his embrace around her, her heart thudded a little faster. What was unrequited was now reciprocated, she could sense.

And holding her, he rushed to the nearest hospital from Huda. Ishaan held her tightly because she wasn't able to stand on her feet. Not once did he fall weak, even when he saw her in a state that could break him completely. He ran to the emergency and asked the doctor to quickly check her. Meanwhile, he called Kavya and told her, "Kavu, your sister really needs to get a hold of herself. She is behaving in the most immature manner that she can. Please take her out of all this yaar."

As he stood outside the emergency ward and the doctor checked her blood sugar and blood pressure, Ishaan was forced to think, '*And I thought her love was immature. If it would have been, she would have moved on months back.*'

'*She's just stupid.*'

As he stood outside and waited for the doctor, he kept cursing himself and Meera for doing all of this to her. He kept pacing up and down when the doctor walked up to him and said, "She has really low blood pressure and too much stress."

Ishaan heard her carefully. "Also, she seems to have slept very less. I asked her the reason, but no answers. Is there any particular reason?"

Ishaan looked embarrassed. Yes, he knew the answer, but when she had kept quiet, even he did. However, in his heart, he knew he was responsible for her to be where she was.

'*This girl is so stubborn and when she fell in love, she would not let it go too,*' he thought, repenting on the way he behaved with her.

Since the last six months, he ensured, they hardly spoke; he made sure that his replies were the most disappointing ones; he tried his level best to distance himself from her, but her love was such that it refused to kneel down and this made him angrily sad.

Ishaan breathed a sigh of relief thinking she was fine, but his eyes didn't. A fat tear drop accumulated in his eyes and dropped down his cheeks. Ishaan, the never so emotional, practical and logical human being was scared. Yes, he had always seen Meera as the one who would get up at 4 and ensure that her work was in place. How could he then see her in such a miserable state? He simply walked outside the hospital and sitting in the parking, he consoled himself, '*She's a fighter and she can come out of this too. She just needs to be strong.*'

As he falsely tried his best to assure his mind, his heart was wrenching with pain on seeing her weak and vulnerable. He knew he never bothered about anyone the way he did for her, but he was now sure of the fact that even if they were together, she wouldn't be able to handle her emotions and would end up messing things further.

'*She's a kid, Ishaan. She just knows how to mess things up. She needs to learn the harder way,*' he told himself and braced himself for facing her after so many days of ignorance as he held her palms and helped her get down the bed. He ensured that her short dress was decently placed and as she got down, he said, sternly, without a trace of any emotion, "I don't think you'll be able to walk in heels. Wear my shoes!"

Meera looked at him and with weakness overflowing from her eyes, she replied, "I am fine. Give me my wedges."

Ishaan said strictly, "Shut up and do not argue! Your stubborn nature already is doing much good to you. Now just listen to me and wear my shoes!"

Putting the shoes in her feet and tying the lace, Ishaan helped her stand on her feet, which she couldn't. The moment Meera kept her feet on the ground, she fell. Ishaan held her from her waist and said, "We will not move an inch till you stand on your feet."

He got a cup of coffee and gave it to her, saying, "Drink this!"

As if a jailor was feeding the thieves in jail, Ishaan sounded as stern as he could. His strictness was his masquerade to hide the weakest side of him which he had seen a moment ago. He was sure that neither of them could be good for each other today and he really wished Meera realised the same as well, but even after everything, she was all there – with the same respect that she had for him.

'*How can she still respect me?*' he questioned himself.

He held the cup and cooled it for her as she sipped slowly. He held her shoulders and kept bracing her back, making her feel comfortable.

Once she was better, they walked till the cab.

Meanwhile, her parents called him asking about her well being. You know, break-ups, heartbreaks, one-sided emotions – everything sounds fancy, but when it comes to falling down and then getting up, think about the two people in your life who can never see you falling. I understand depression exists, but to fight it, the only support that you will have is from your parents. Never let them down. Never!

As Meera slept with her head on his lap, not once did he bother to stroke her hair, even when his heart again and again instructed him to do so. He simply looked out as she slept peacefully in his lap. For a minute, as the cab passed India Gate, Ishaan felt like giving her a tight hug and telling her that her worth was much more than what she was doing to herself, but like always, he stopped himself.

'*You can block a person from Facebook, WhatsApp, Instgram, SnapChat and Hangouts, but how do you block that person from your heart?*' he asked himself, looking at her.

As they entered her flat, he helped her sleep on her bed and told Kavya, "Take care of her. She needs you."

Kavya in turn replied, "No! She needs you."

Ishaan stopped as he replied, "That's what I want to delete from her life – getting attached to people without a reason, respecting them much more than they deserve and being head over heels present for people who don't even deserve her. If going through all this helps, then maybe it's meant to be, Kavu."

Giving her a hug, Ishaan left in the darkness to reach his place, and as he walked towards the metro station, everything flashed in his mind – the chatter, the banter, the smile that she always carried, her cribbing, her tantrums and her positivity. In that moment, he prayed for her career to sail her through this time as well, and in the hope of her being fine, he left.

◆

At 3 a.m., Meera got up, startled.

"I really love you, Ishaan," she said. Kavya, who was wide-eyed awake near her sister, heard what she said. Undoubtedly, she was extremely worried for Meera.

She pacified Meera and said, "Di, sleep!"

She stroked her elder sister's hair as Meera said, "Kavu, I want to talk to him once..."

And that is when Kavya lost her cool. She got up, switched

on the light and asked Meera to sit straight as she shouted, "*What is wrong with you?*"

"You've been fucking up a lot of things. High time now, and trust me, Meera – I will not take any of this shit anymore. You love him, right?"

Kavya looked straight into Meera's eyes and said, "*You love him.* So? What do we do now? Beg for his love for you? Or, do you want me to go and kidnap him and then make him commit to you?"

Meera struggled to say, "No…"

"Wait, I am talking!" Kavya stopped her.

"Yes, so, what do we do? To make you back to normal, what should I do? I'll simply blackmail him and say my sister is a bloody coward and she cannot handle her life by herself. She needs you. You want me to do this to you and him, is it? Wait, let's call him."

Kavya was about to swipe on his name to call him, when Meera stopped her, "I don't want to force my feelings on him."

"And, what else have you been doing all these days? You think he's enjoying his life with you being such a miserable jerk? Di, accept the fact that he *does not love you*. It is as simple as these four words. How hard is it for you to believe, yaar?"

"And, even if he does. How does that matter if I have to bring my sister back from a hospital because she has sworn to behave like an idiot?" Kavya added.

"Do you think I am an immature person?" Meera asked.

"I don't see being expressive as being immature. I don't see being full of life as being immature and I don't see you as an immature person. I've seen you fighting so hard for yourself, how could you be someone immature? But, yes, you are being immature by not accepting the fact that things are just not meant to be between the two of you. You need to accept this and then accept yourself the way you are. How does it even matter what Ishaan thinks? What matters is what you think. Remember, if it is meant to be, it will happen – no matter what."

As Kavya said so, she added, "And, I've just registered you for a three-day trip to Shimla. It is beautiful. Go and enjoy it!"

Whatever her younger sister said had an immediate impact on Meera and she removed Ishaan from all her social media handles immediately, not escaping his gaze, but just helping her life get a new perspective, which perhaps was above them and above her. Sometimes, holding on to someone is a good option, but when that bond starts deteriorating from both ends, why stretch it to worsen the situation?

When you know things are not working out even after putting considerable efforts, just let go of them. Even at that moment, she knew that there was a spark between the two of them and she could see that pain in his eyes, but just because holding to it wouldn't positively help anyone of them, Meera stepped back.

She did not want a cliff hanging ending for the two of them. She demanded closure, which she did not get, but she could create her own closure, right? And yes, she did.

At that moment, only the trip seemed to stay in her mind.

'Life is a happy place, Meera.'

Beauty never lies in the eyes of the viewer, but in the perspective of that viewer. And at times, even when you don't have that perspective, it is important to take a step out of the troublesome zone, to find it.

Meera had already been going through a lot in the last six months. Especially after the hospital anti-climax, she needed some break from the monotony of her life – some time away from the metros, the metro stations, the office cafeteria and Ishaan's presence. Kavya had correctly identified the vacation place for her sister - Shimla.

And through her WhatsApp statuses, Kavya knew her sister was living in that moment. Meera posted pictures from Narkanda, Kufri and the Mall Road. From the glow of her face, Kavya knew it was not only the place but also a completely new company that Meera was opening to.

To know how she was, Kavya called her.

"Chep, *kaisi hai?*" she asked.

Meera, who at that moment was climbing the trek for Jakhoo

temple, took the phone and replied, with huffs and puffs, "Hi Kavu. Right now, we are climbing to Jakhoo temple. It's said that people who complete the trek in less than thirty minutes are extremely fit, the ones who take forty-five minutes are fit and then rest all of them are unfit."

Kavya laughed and asked, "And since when have you been climbing?"

"Sixty-eight minutes. But, it's not my fault. I started and then I got digressed with the beauty of this city and then, I started clicking pictures and then, I found a dog that was adorable and taking snap videos, I lost my way."

Kavya continuously laughed at the free amusement she received from her sister after a very long time.

"Then, as I was walking, an uncle told me to remove my specs. Who does that? I won't remove my specs," Meera complained as she was able to see her trek leader.

"You know, Utkarsh completed the trek in exactly twenty minutes."

"Mountains are his love. He obviously would," Kavya said, being truly herself.

She added, "Good that you are back to your normal self, so that I too can be carefree, unlike the stupid mature I had to become for you."

As Meera was about to respond, a monkey jumped from the right side and sat on her right shoulder, snatching her spectacles. Meera was about to shout when she remembered that 'no, be calm with animals'. Ishaan used to tell her every time she shrieked on seeing a dog.

As she calmly stood, the monkey too was of her breed – stubborn. Each character in this story is stubborn, I tell you!

He kept snatching her specs and Meera kept holding tightly to them and to the tourists, it was 'free ka entertainment'. As

Utkarsh, her trek lead saw the tiff from a distance, he asked everyone in their team to stay away.

He had been observing Meera since they started for the trip and knowing whatever he knew from his observation, he knew she would be fine.

"She's a problem solver. Let her solve it on her own," he said, confidently, pacifying his team.

One of his assistants tried to say something, to which Utkarsh replied, "What will happen? She'll get some scratches on her face, right? Let her handle it. I think she will enjoy this adventure."

For a while, the monkey and Meera had a cold fight. But then, she left her specs, saving her face. The monkey did a little dab, after which he jumped on a pine tree. Meera ran behind him, pleading him to return her specs.

Utkarsh saw all of this from a distance and laughed at the imperfect creature Meera was – she would fall, get up, fall again and then get up again – all by herself. Yes, she messed up things, but she ensured she brought them back to normal. As he saw her, she was throwing Parle G biscuits, some sweets, whatever Frooti tetra packs she had as a bribe for the monkey to return her specs.

As she stood below a tall pine tree, the monkey climbed up and teased her, as if telling her that he was and is better than her. I think he was showcasing his monkey-swag when Meera folded her hands and threw some sweets at him. Smartly, he came down and grabbed them and then, holding the specs as carefully as his heart, ran up again, with a smirk on his face.

Meera smiled and laughed the way she had almost forgotten to and laughing and enjoying the experience, she brought more biscuits. Somehow, after all her pleading, the monkey dropped her specs, but – there's a 'but' here. He dropped broken spectacles.

Initially, Meera wanted to crib about it, but the next moment, she looked at her shoe laces. She wore fancy sneakers and taking out her lace, she did some engineering with it and tied it around her specs, making them wearable. She then clicked a selfie, smiling broadly and posted it for her followers, with the caption:

'Finding out alternatives is what life is all about. #Shimla #TrekkingDiaries'

And then, she completed her trek to find a happy trek lead waiting for her as others went inside the temple and had lunch.

Utkarsh was a twenty-five-year-old traveller who had just started his startup, named 'Travel Diaries'. The idea behind his startup was to lead treks with corporate employees and ensure they have a trek, which wasn't just one among many. He made them take the tougher path to the easier destination. While the other groups would take a normal route, he would always make his own route and then ask his team to walk the tougher path.

Wasn't he like Ishaan? Even he wanted to walk the tougher path, so that life becomes all the more adventurous for him and his companion.

Coming back to Shimla, Utkarsh gave Meera a high five and said, "I was sure you would come as cheerfully as you did. I somewhere knew you were a sport."

Meera smiled, proudly showing her specs to him. "I know, I saw you fighting with the monkey. It was war in itself, no?" he said, sarcastically.

As they walked towards the temple, Meera said, "I am so glad you didn't intervene, Utkarsh. I loved sorting this out myself."

He smiled back as they sat in one of the serene corners of the temple. Lord Hanuman's gigantic statue blessed the city beautifully as Meera said, "Sometimes, it's not anything else, but just our apprehensions that limit us from going beyond the boundaries we set for ourselves."

Utkarsh smiled and then, he smirked a bit. Meera looked at him and asked what was going on in his mind, to which, he replied, "You know what?"

"What?" she asked, inquisitive.

"I checked your Facebook profile when we were in the bus and I was really impressed by your blogs and write-ups."

Meera smiled, registering the fact that someone who she was inspired from appreciated her work. In a little span of time, Utkarsh's attitude inspired her to be carefree. It wasn't dramatic, but sometimes, you are just influenced by some people and their personality. For Meera, Utkarsh was that person.

She said, "Okay, and…?"

She waited as he replied, "And, I figured out two things. One, you are a great and extremely talented writer. I loved the campaign you did for Manyavar."

She heard him carefully. "And, second?" she asked.

"Second is that since the last twenty days, whatever you have posted is about one topic – one-sided love and pain."

Meera smiled sheepishly.

"I know it's personal but I just felt like telling you that you are one wonderful person, Meera. Maybe, the person you love is even better, but destiny is as stubborn as you are. Let it go." He explained.

Travel has its own charm, and travellers have the most experienced stories ever. Utkarsh's travel sponsored his stories, listening to which, Meera said, "I do realise that. I could have deleted these blogs but I deliberately did not remove them. If someone has been a part of your life, why even think of deleting that phase – no matter how good or bad it has been, it is yours."

As carefree as the breeze was, Utkarsh asked casually, "So, a broken heart speaks?"

"Of course not. My heart is fully fine. It's just happily loving the person it wants to love."

"What do you mean?" he asked, relaxing.

Meera opened her hair, which were tied in a messy bun and with the calm breeze of the atmosphere brushing their faces, she replied, "When you fall in love, you expect that your partner would be with you and such thoughts tend to stay in your mind. But, as you realise the worth of love, expectations start leaving. I loved someone and I genuinely loved him. But, I just expected too much in return. I made a trillion mistakes to run behind him. You know Utkarsh, I actually felt like a sales person being ignored by a potential customer at times."

He laughed and added, "India's popular fashion blogger felt so? This is news. Let me record it."

Meera laughed as she continued, "I forgot that it was love and love is never supposed to be rushed with. It will sway its own way and will take its own twists and turns to make a place in my life."

Utkarsh heard her silently, and then added, "Absolutely! Your worth is decided by the respect you have for your own perspective."

"Right! And you know what the best part about love is? No one is wrong and both of us were right. Ishaan never said he loved me. It wasn't his fault, right? And I kept expecting him to return as a friend at least, failing to understand how difficult it would be for him," Meera said, letting the breeze paint beautiful images with the wind and trees in front of her eyes.

"And, till it's true, nothing really matters. I love him as much as I did when I told it to him. Or actually a little more."

When she completed what she was saying, Utkarsh asked, "The fact that your love might never return doesn't scare you?"

"Of course it does. But, when love is your strength, patience and acceptance accompanies it," she replied confidently.

Sitting there, Utkarsh looked at his watch and once he knew he had time, he narrated, "When you travel a lot, you get to experience different situations. You know, when I travelled recently to Spiti Valley, there were situations I really did not know how to react to. Sometimes, there would be extreme excitement and sometimes, nothing else but depression of being isolated. But, in between everything, one fact was a constant – my love for completing the trek. As travellers, we always say that no matter what happens, finish your trek."

Meera listened to him, trying to find the connection to her story, which he did mention in the next second. "In life too, there will be thousand issues. Sometimes personal, sometimes professional. What's important is to keep moving ahead and leave the burden of the last step behind. If you carry all the traces of your steps, how will you climb higher? The lighter, the better."

Meera smiled broadly and added, "Of course. But, I can't leave Ishaan behind. My love for him was a little beyond togetherness. Yes, I can stop pestering him, at least."

Utkarsh smirked and said, "Of course, I don't know about you, but I wouldn't tolerate anyone ignoring my friend."

And in that second, Meera felt like the breeze was taking something away from her. As the breeze got louder and faster, she could feel more of it leaving her, she could sense herself being lighter. Maybe the atmosphere at Jakhoo temple took away the burden of what Meera was burdening herself with. Maybe, it was negativity that the air took away from her; maybe, the burden of underestimating herself; maybe, it was just a phase that the breeze took away from her and silently replaced it with space to welcome new memories.

Meera felt free and in that air; she enjoyed her freedom. She realised that she was always a free bird – and becoming one carefree creature once again, she felt she was welcoming her own older self. Well, no one else but she had caged her thoughts and limited them to one single relationship. Oh definitely, that relationship was an asset in her life, but the emotions became a liability she was trying to get rid of.

Truly, her eyes still loved him and her smile still respected him. I would hence repeat, '*The people who love are the luckiest and those who fall in one-sided love are the strongest.*'

Meera really needs to grow up?

When Meera returned from Shimla, she was happier and closer to the version she was earlier. She was cheerful, happy and energetic. Yes, she travelled through the same routes, but this time, Ishaan's memory was her strength and not her weakness. As she wrote her blogs, they didn't talk about leaving love midway, but they spoke about how love could be her strength.

Ishaan, on the other hand, was perturbed. He had tried his level best to convince himself that he did not love Meera, but whenever he was alone, all he could think was about Meera. He tried going out with friends, who he got bored with, because they were too mature for him, he felt. He tried walking out of his comfort zone and went to skate as well, but once again, he got bored because there was no adventure happening in his life.

Now that he was habitual of being the centre of people's smiles in the metro, he felt empty when he travelled alone, standing quietly. And frustrated with the feeling of trying to figure out what he wanted from life, he called Kavya, his problem solver.

"Hi Kavya," he said.

Kavya, busy looking at her sister's photographs, replied pretty happily, "Hi bhaiya. How are you?"

"I don't know," he said.

"Okay! What is it that you don't know?" she asked, pretty chilled out. She knew Ishaan was always clear about what he wanted. She was so sure of her brother.

"I don't know Kavya. I am just feeling too annoyed and frustrated. I like being quiet. It's not that anyway I used to talk like a loudspeaker, but now that I am quiet, I find silence a little burdening. Then, when I travel, I used to travel silently, without stories or adventures, but these days, I find my life monotonous and boring and just empty. As if I am a box, which is emptied of all its substance. You know what I am trying to say, right?"

Kavya replied, "Of course not, bhaiya. Even if *you* hear what you were saying, you wouldn't understand a single word."

Ishaan was quiet. Kavya continued, "What is it? I haven't seen you contemplating over something as much as you are doing today. Plus, you sound nervous. Is everything okay?"

"Yes and no," he replied.

"Everything is definitely not okay. I feel I am not talking to you, but to Meera," Kavya said.

"Meera..." Ishaan repeated.

"Yes, my sister. I hope you haven't forgotten her yet," Kavya smirked.

"She's not someone who you can forget anyway, Kavu," Ishaan said.

Kavya smiled and then there was a brief pause, after which, Ishaan said, "Kavya, I think I am in love."

Kavya was startled, to say the least. Love and Ishaan – a weird combination to imagine for her. She asked, "And, with?"

"Of course, your sister," he replied.

Kavya jumped up with excitement, but some apprehensions too. She said, "I think Meera has just walked out of a zone where she cannot take more emotions, bhaiya. I am afraid, let's let her be."

Ishaan replied, "I know I have made situations such that love became a weakness for her. I promise I would make it her strength now. That's what love is supposed to be, right?"

Kavya heard what he said and then told him, "Tell her then."

Ishaan asked, "How?"

Kavya, being Kavya, replied, "Figure that out yourself. Did you ask me before ignoring her?" She smirked and kept the phone, leaving Ishaan with thoughts about facing Meera.

He felt lighter after accepting what he felt, but he was extremely nervous. *How would he express it?*

Epilogue

As he stood at the door, wearing a black shirt and trousers, looking dapper, his hair were ruffled, the way she liked them and his smile was as innocent as she loved. While he was about to press the doorbell, Meera was busy finalising for a session that she had in NIFD a day after.

Wearing a Mickey Mouse dress on her, she was busy dancing to the tunes of the latest Bollywood numbers, when Kavya opened the door.

"You look smart, bhaiya," she said as she smirked.

Ishaan walked till Meera's room and as he saw Meera dancing and working, he was sure that the earlier version of the same girl was back.

'I unnecessarily wanted her to grow up. She's perfect the way she is. And who the hell was I to tell her if she needed to be mature or not? If she's successful being who she is, she is perfect,' he thought.

Meera, who was pretty chilled out in dancing to the *dhinchak* tunes, surprisingly wasn't shocked looking at him. She happily waved at him and putting her music system on pause, she walked towards him.

Every step that she took towards him, his heartbeat thudded a little louder, and the moment she came close to him, he said what he had been thinking in the last few hours, "See, I know I am the trouble maker and you are the problem solver. I also know that I had no right to leave your life and just make a guest appearance. And I had no right to ask you to grow up or not. It is your life and completely your choice. Plus, I was an idiot to think that someone who is cheerful would be kiddish. You know I was never stereotypical, but just lost track when your career came in my mind. I forgot that it was your choice to manage it with a relationship and I wasn't anyone to be a guardian for you. I am sorry. In fact, love is not leaving someone for them to achieve their dreams, but to be together and make that dream yours so that you achieve it together. Let's make this dream work together. I was stupid when I thought I would distract you. Maybe, I become the focus for you to write?"

Meera smiled as her sister looked at the two of them from a distance.

"You know I am bad with emotions, right? So, I'll just tell you straightforward that I love you and I love you the way you are – in the Mickey Mouse dress, with the most cheerful voice, with the worst pick-up lines, with the lamest jokes you'll make. It was never you who needed me, but I am the one who needs you. You were never immature, you were just being yourself. I was wrong when I told you to grow up. Today, I tell you to never grow up, Meera."

Meera looked into his eyes, and she undoubtedly saw true love. She had always seen it and for the first time, she could feel those eyes talking to hers. She deeply acknowledged those feelings and smiled as broadly as she could.

◆

What do you think she said?
Kahaani abhi baaki hai mere dost...

By the same author

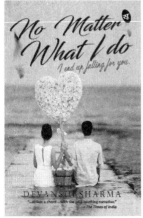

NO MATTER WHAT I DO

Kabir, Amaira, Kushank and Suhani – four very different people bound together by love and friendship, are struggling to find the motto of their lives. Four individuals striving to find themselves. Four threads entangled together and four lives recuperating each other – *No Matter What I Do* is the story of these four youngsters, on a journey to find the true meaning of their lives and love.

The love story narrates tales of reversing stereotypes and finding individuality. But will they really find their reason to live?

IMPERFECT MISFITS

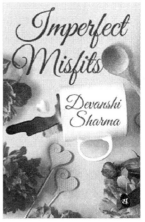

Just like a scoop of vanilla ice cream makes the sizzling chocolate brownie delicious, these best friends complimented each other. A chef by passion, Tiasha jumps and waves through her professional choices, while Aakaash, the witty stand-up comedian, knows exactly what he wants.

Imperfect Misfits is a story of two perfect misfits, a whole lot of food, frolic, emotions and their endless imperfections. The question is – will their friendship survive through this wavy journey of love?